Petra,
    Such a ple_____ _____ ___
You are so beautiful. Call me
 When you are ready to
   write!
                                    Love
                                    Steph

MW01124025

# *TURF* *WARS*

A Gametime Series Novel

## STEPHANIE SINKFIELD

Turf Wars is dedicated to the two most important men in my life, Gerald and Xavier Sinkfield!

**Books by Stephanie Sinkfield**

Shoot the Lights Out

Turf Wars

**The Virtuous Wife**

**Proverbs 31: 10-31**

*Who can find a virtuous wife? For her worth is far above rubies.*

# Acknowledgements

I had a ball writing Shoot the Lights Out! The book really helped me mourn the death of my father, Thomas Brown, who was an amazing man, yet celebrate the life that he helped breath in to me some 40 years ago.

While writing Shoot the Lights Out, Keeva, really started to form a life of her own. She is fearless, beautiful, whip smart, has no filter, and is every woman! And how could we leave Amos out of the picture! Many people have asked me if the characters in my book represent people in my life. While I will never admit that they do, any writer would be lying if they didn't admit that art imitates life!

I want to thank the Phat Girls who include my mom, Ellen Brown, my sisters Shelbie Hugle and Kimberly Gibson-Harris, and my niece Ashlee Harris for always having my back. And my sister friends who read Turf Wars in its roughest form and gave me honest feedback: Melinda Bone, Nicole Brown, Karlene Claridy, Beverly Muse, Ursula Richardson-Bizzle, Tahnika Rodriguez, and Patricia Smith. Also thanks to Brittney Officer and Michael Williams, my team for holding it down! And the many friends, family, book clubs and avid readers that supported my first book also deserve a huge thank you!

Dody Riggs, Visually Appetizing, and Claridy Communications, thank you for helping me breathe life into my books! These small business owners have been a God send with editing, graphic arts, and publishing!

And as always my husband Gerald Sinkfield, BKA Sink, I cannot thank you and Rodney Hugle, my brother enough for helping me with football terms...even though you had no idea you were during the writing of Turf Wars and for supporting my writing. I love you!

I hope you enjoy Turf Wars, the second book in my Gametime Series. Give me feedback at inSinkpress.com, Facebook, Amazon, Nook, and Goodreads!

# Contents

# The Year of the Keeva!

I can't believe Jackie lost our earrings! Now I have just 30 minutes to pick up a new pair at the jewelry store before I have to be at the church for the renewal of the vows. But wait, I'm getting ahead of myself. Better back up just a bit so I can bring everybody up to date.

More than a year ago, my first cousin Jackie's father passed away. Uncle Shorty, Coach Donovan to most, was the king not only of Seymour High School but of the city of Nashville. In his 25 years as a coach he won 13 state basketball championships—one of the winningest high school coaches in state history. Uncle Shorty was loved by people from around the world, and his death left a gaping hole in the city of Nashville, Seymour High School, and the hearts of our family members. Uncle Shorty and my Aunt Ella were married for like a million years and produced two girls, and they adopted my cousin Leo when he was just a baby.

Jackie moved back home from Seattle after Uncle Shorty's funeral, and eventually she assumed his coaching duties. She also literally fell into the loving arms of pro football player Adaris Singleton. After a fairytale (if occasionally rocky) courtship, Adaris proposed to Jackie with a flawless four-carat Tiffany diamond ring right in the study of the dream home he had built for her. Obviously she accepted.

Now, just four months after the proposal, we are in the 11th hour, as the couple is about to renew their vows. You see, they couldn't wait to consummate their relationship, so last month they snuck off to a little resort in the Bahamas called The Atlantis and got married. It worked out really well for the two of them, if you get my drift but not so much for all of us they left back in Nashville preparing their wedding reception for some 300 people.

After Adaris proposed to Jackie, her sister Serena—Rena to all of us—and their mother, Ella, started planning this elaborate wedding. Right in the middle of their planning, Jackie made the grand announcement that she didn't want to go through the pomp and circumstance of picking out a wedding dress, a venue, or anything else. Even after Rena assured her that all of the above had already been done and deposits had been made, Jackie put her size 9 Louboutin foot down and insisted that any plans being made would be for a reception only. After my Aunt Ella picked her chin up off the floor and Serena finished her pouting, the three of us agreed that we would create the best wedding reception we could.

Our family really needed a celebration after the "Year of the Shorty," a name coined by Jackie to describe a year filled with death, retirements, budding career moves, new relationships, and a lot of self-discovery. Jackie decided to retire from her position as a WNBA player in Seattle and move

2

home. The principal of Seymour High School, who was one of my uncle's good friends, hoodwinked her into taking the low-paying coaching position leading 13 stinky, horny teenage boys with the help of a pipsqueak know-it-all assistant because he knew that, much like Unc, Jackie would turn those lemons into lemonade. And in fact she made them into the Chick-fil-A lemonade—in other words, fabulous! She pulled off a 24-8 season, lost by one point in the sub-state tournament, and made the whole damn team fall in love with her . . . along with one team member's daddy. Yes, one of her players just so happened to be Adaris Jr, son of the aforementioned Adaris Singleton.

Adaris Sr recently retired from the Tennessee Trailblazers football team at the ripe young age of 32. Throughout his career he won every award known to man with the word "pro" in front of it, except the Super Bowl title. You should have seen him and Jackie as they danced around and tried to deny the love they had for each other. They in fact fell for each other the very day Uncle Shorty died, as Jackie was rushing through the Nashville airport on her way home. Well, I should say that Jackie fell, literally . . . she tripped over some obese chick, and while her big ass was sitting on the floor of the terminal she laid eyes on Adaris for the very first time.

After that infamous fall, Adaris was drawn to Jackie like a moth to a flame. He ardently wooed and courted her—that is, until he found out that Jackie was coaching his son. Once he knew that, everything between them was put on hold. Well, except for a few interludes which yours truly helped to orchestrate. However, the Chief Orchestrator in Charge just so happened to be Aunt Ella, who could put *Black Singles Meet* out of business. She was so smooth about it that even Adaris and Jackie didn't know what was going on half the damn time!

During their long courtship, Jackie held on to her goodies, which I am convinced helped induce Adaris to produce the four-carat bling-bling. While I admire Jackie's purity, I think they must have broken the mold when she came along—a sister like me could definitely not have resisted Adaris' charms!

His charms . . . but I digress! So, the "Year of the Shorty" is now over, and I've declared it the "Year of the Keeva!" As soon as I pick up these earrings and make it through the reception, I am getting on a plane to go somewhere where I won't have to deal with love, weddings, and happy ever after's. Well, at least not until Chris proposes to Max.

You see, I was doing just fine. I was getting into a groove with my company, KeMarketing, where my focus is on helping businesses develop marketing and communication strategies to increase revenues. A few years ago I was working as a VP for a Fortune 100 company and making them money hand over fist, and I got sick of the grind. I was working for "the

4

man," making him billions of dollars a year, and "he" was acting like he was doing me a favor. I turned my back on the six figures they were paying me and told them to take their job and shove it! Well, I didn't say that because I am a lady, but during my exit interview I made sure that I told them how a sister felt about being used.

I haven't looked back since the day I walked out of that 20-story building. I felt the same sense of liberation as I did the day I walked out on my ex-husband, Damon McGhee, when I caught him cheating on me for the fifth time . . . that I knew of. I stomped out of the house like I was six feet tall, with *I'm Every Woman* blasting from the stereo. In reality I am a petite wisp of a thing unless I have my stilettos on. I walked out on him and into my own company, my own crib, and my own world!

A woman can only take so much shit. You give your love to a man you think loves you back. You repeat vows in front of hundreds of people about being faithful to each other, and then he decides to renege on his promise. Damon and I got married young. He was my first real boyfriend. I was strutting my stuff as I walked across the Tennessee State University campus in my pink and green my sophomore year, and there he was. I played hard to get for about two weeks, and after that we were inseparable. Three months after we graduated we were married, and soon after that several girls I suspected

5

he was messing with in college became his chicks on the side. You see, youth makes you forgive because you think that things will change.

Well, they didn't change, and finally I didn't want to play his game any longer with my va jay jay so I grew up quick. During our fifth wedding anniversary dinner I had my attorney do what Damon had been doing to me for years. I embarrassed his ass by serving him with a singing "divorce-a-gram." One of my newest clients had come up with the concept, and I figured I might as well try it out to see if my new marketing plan was effective. And I must say, it worked like a charm. In fact, after Damon stomped out of the restaurant, several people came over to ask for a referral. I have since helped my client make millions—minus my 10 percent, of course.

It took a little over a year to finalize our divorce. Thankfully we didn't have any children. My spirit just wouldn't allow me to take that step. There are already enough jacked-up children in this world, why should I add to it by giving my child a cheating baby daddy? Believe me, I did not go into our marriage thinking we would divorce. I know that God hates divorce and I do too. It's like a death, and everyone is affected by it. You have to split up your household and everything you own, and even your friends and family have to pick sides. (I must admit, there were a few family members on my side that

6

I gladly let Damon have, because they got on my damn nerves.) But after finding him in my house with one of his hoes, I decided that I was not going to live in a hell on earth. Since we married so young and didn't have many assets, all I asked the judge for was the money I had in my checking account and to be released from any debts. I was willing to give up the material things to gain my freedom. So I got my freedom, but I also came to realize that freedom comes with a cost.

In my case the cost is being a bridesmaid once again (well, almost), which brings me back to why I am driving down Westend Avenue to get these damn earrings. Jackie decided to give all of her "almost" bridesmaids a pair of beautiful diamond hoop earrings to wear at the reception. I secretly think she is trying to con us for not being pissed about their elopement. Believe me, it's working, especially since I am about to buy myself an upgraded pair. Jackie thought she gave our earrings to Rena to bring to the hotel, but she can't find them. When she told Adaris, he calmly got me on the phone and said, "Hey Keev, can you meet Amos in the lobby to get my credit card and go get some more earrings? I don't want my baby to be stressed out about anything today." He didn't say buy the same pair of earrings did he?

Now, did I say that Adaris is a charming MF? Well, I lied. I did think he was charming until he said to meet Amos in the lobby. I don't plan to meet Amos anywhere anytime soon if I can help it. Amos Hunter, the starting center of the Tennessee Trailblazers, is the bane of my existence! It all started last September when I went to a football game with Jackie and Max, who is Jackie's best gal pal. That scene was like a bad episode of *Girlfriends*, because at the time Adaris and Jackie were estranged. Every woman who wanted to be Mrs. Singleton, including the real Mrs. Singleton (Adaris' mother), was in the owner's box gunning for him to put a ring on it.

As I was saying before, Adaris and Jackie had taken a time out from their romance dance, since Jackie was coaching Adaris' son. But the gang decided to reunite to watch Adaris and Chris play each other in the Tennessee stadium. Adaris' friend Chris Map plays for the Giants. Last fall, Jackie's best friend Max had come into town from St. Croix. It seems that during a night at BB King's Blues Club, Chris fell head over hills for Max and her feet—yeah, he has a bit of a foot fetish. Max decided she liked him back, which is saying something, because she doesn't like most people.

Anywho, back to the owner's box. During the game Max and I realized that several women there were gunning for Adaris. To cope with the competition Jackie decided to drink, but she can't hold her liquor worth a damn, so after about five glasses of Pinot she was three sheets to the wind. Adaris invited us to his hotel room for dinner after the game. Being the proverbial third wheel I thought about not going, but with Jackie drunk and me her only next of kin at the game, I decided to go along for the ride. Well, and for the free food—you know football players really like to eat and eat well!

You know what happens when there is an extra girl at a party. They invite an extra boy, and this time said extra boy just happened to be Amos. I recognized the familiar faces when the men walked into the room, except one. He was a 6 foot 7, 350-pound man who looked like a combination of Ray Lewis and Shaquille O'Neil, only much cuter. Now I am petite on a day when my posture is good and just plain short when it's bad. So this guy came in and right away invaded my personal space—frankly, he scared me to death! Then he had the nerve to act like a male Tamar Braxton and speak in the third person. He ate his dinner and Jackie's—she got sick after the five glasses of Pinot—then he offered to take me home in my own limo and asked if he could make it rain! After politely telling him he didn't have enough money in his pocket for me to assume the position, if you get my drift, I let him take me home.

Since that night, Amos has been on my jock! He calls me, he sends me love letters, he cooks for me, and he has asked me countless times to meet his Mama who, judging by the pictures, is just as huge as he is. Any normal woman would love all the attention, but not me. I am a skeptic, suspicious and untrusting. And I am not available. After the divorce I decided to be and remain a free agent. Free to do whatever the hell I want to do when I get good and ready. I like men short, tall, cute, ugly, young, and . . . well, not old, because my Aunt D says old men give you worms. I like the fact that I can choose to choose whomever I choose and am very comfortable with my singleness. That is, until I see couples like Adaris and Jackie and Rena and Micah, who really seem to enjoy being together.

Amos' intent is to get married and have children—in short, to tie me down. Been there and done that, at least up to the children, and I am just not into it at this point. Don't get me wrong, Amos is a wonderful man. He loves the Lord, he loves his big Mama, he is loyal to his friends, and he is a great football player. So what is wrong with him you ask? Besides the fact that he is big as hell, loud as hell, and too clingy, nothing! He is a gentle giant and surprisingly very light on his feet, considering that he is so damn big. We have been going back and forth for months now, and by all accounts he is not giving up. Of course I know I am the bomb, but most men give up and move on after being rejected so many times.

So, you can see why my excitement about going to the jewelry store with someone else's money came to a screeching halt when Amos' name came up. I expected to see his big butt at the reception, but there I would be safe in the company of about 298 other people, not in a small room where he would have another chance to wear me down. I am just not in the mood to feel all lovey dovey and mushy today. I want to dance with someone who won't make me look like a midget and get my jam on! After all, the best place to meet your next date is at a wedding reception. You do not take sand to the beach—and in this case, Amos was the entire beach.

So I politely say to Adaris, "No, I will not meet Amos to get your credit card. Besides, its bad luck for the almost groomsman to see the just about bridesmaid before the reception. What the hell do you think they created bellhops for? Get one to bring it to me! And hurry up, times a wastin'. And I hope you know that to compensate for my time I am going to get myself a bigger pair of earrings than Max's and Rena's."

"Oh yeah, I forgot about that timeless tradition, Keeva. How about I have Chris bring the credit card so he can sneak a peek at Max's feet. Does that work better?"

"You bet your fine ass it does. Thanks Adaris. I knew Jackie had picked a winner, and not just because you are handsome and rich."

"Thanks Keeva. Tell my baby I will see her in a few minutes."

"Yeah whatever, and thanks for understanding, Adaris."

"You're welcome, cuz."

# The Rules of the Game

As I'm riding down West End Avenue, I think back to a conversation Jackie and I once had about love and dating, and I distinctly remember telling her my philosophy: Dating means you are spending time getting to know someone, maybe having dinner, going to the movies, or whatever. Dating does not mean you are in a relationship. I decided after my divorce from Damon that I would date like a man. If I see you and something about you interests me, then I might allow you to spend time with me. We can hang out and get to know each other. It means we have made a commitment to see where things go. But it doesn't necessarily mean we will be intimate. If we decide together that we want to take things to another level, then we will.

If things start getting too heavy, it's my cue to move on. I am not ready for a commitment. I did that with Damon for six years, and he didn't hold up his end of the deal. I told myself when I became single again that I would take my time dating until I found the person who was the best fit for me. And I have met some great men. Some have been well off, some have been poor as hell. Some were beautiful and some were ugly. Some had great careers, others were jobless—hey, I am an equal opportunity woman. If one thing about a guy intrigues me I will give myself a chance to get to know him.

But until I find that one person who, as Stevie Wonder would say, knocks me off my feet, I am going to play it that way. I make my own rules.

So, as I sit in my car in front of the jewelry store, already running late, I start to question those dating rules. Who in the hell do I think I'm kidding by saying I only want to date? What dingbat walks around saying she doesn't want a commitment? Me, that's who. Why? Because I am terrified that someone is going to sneak up on my heart and hurt me . . . again.

One thing I have figured out is that most men have an agenda from the moment you meet them. They put you in one of three categories: friend, dalliance, or wifey. I would much rather dictate which slot I'm in, which is unequivocally the dalliance category. But Amos skipped me ahead toward the wifey category very quickly, and that scares the hell out of me. If I had met him earlier in my life I would strongly consider settling down, but I'm gun shy now. It's just very hard for me to trust that a man will be loyal. Love doesn't come in a neat little package. In fact, it often comes in a jacked-up brown box that has tattered corners and a hole in the bottom.

*** 

"What did she say, Dair?" Amos asks with a hopeful look.

"She told me that she would see you at the reception, Dog."

"Tell me the truth man! She said she doesn't want to see me, didn't she?"

"She didn't say those words exactly. She actually said it was bad luck for her to see the just about groomsmen before the reception whatever that means."

"Leave it to Keeva to make up some crap like that. But since most people meet their wifey at a wedding reception, she may be on to something, man. I can wait another hour to see her. I've already gone an entire week."

"That's the optimistic Amos I know. Always seeing the good in even the most jacked-up situation," World says with a huge laugh.

"That's the only way I can survive this madness called Keeva. I have had some challenges in my day, but that little woman is about to drive me nuts."

"Well, let's have a toast to the fool." World raises his glass.

"What he meant to say is let's have a toast to the food, my man," says Adaris. "I asked the caterer to put some of your favorite items at the food stations."

"I hate to agree with World on anything, but I am starting to think I am a damn fool. I have asked Keeva a hundred times to give us a chance to get to know each other and she keeps telling me no. But I know in my heart that she is the woman I am destined to be with," says Amos.

"Then don't give up on her man. You know what Jackie and I had to go through to get to this point in our lives. It wasn't easy, and at one point I didn't think our love could survive the aftermath of her dad's death, her taking on his coaching role, my child, or our careers. But I love the fact that it wasn't easy. Don't get me wrong, loving her is hella easy, but all the stuff around us can really mess with things. And remember, when you marry someone you get the whole damn family. Jackie's is teeming with ex-cons, addicts, and overachievers. Oh, yeah, that's right—you are in love with one of them!"

"Keeva is an ex-con!?" Amos yells. "I knew something was up with her. She is always looking over her shoulder and never sits with her back to the door when she lets me take her out to dinner!"

"Calm down, dude. I don't think Dair was talking about Keeva being an ex-con, were you man?" says World.

"No, stupid—well, at least not that I know of. But I've only been in the Donovan family for a few weeks now, so I am sure there are a few skeletons I don't know about yet," Adaris teases. "But for me it doesn't matter what Jackie's family has going on. I married her for better or for worse, and my prayer is that we are heading to better. Sure we have a few unresolved things," he adds with a grin, "but we're a team and we can work through those things together."

Shelley says to Amos, "Sounds like when you finally get to see Keeva tonight you need to ask her some questions about her past. Maybe getting to know more about her will help you build your future."

Amos looks at his married friend. "Well Shelley, since you are the married man in the circle, Amos will take your advice. Maybe he needs to slow down a little bit and stop focusing on being where Tiffany and you are and work on being her friend."

"Don't take any advice from me my man," says World with a chuckle. "I'm still working on getting Max to commit to a long-distance relationship. And I do have an idea how both you and Keeva feel. I married the wrong woman the first time and she scarred me for life. Now that I have found the right one, I fear she may scar me for life ."

Adaris decides to add his 10 cents' worth. "And I would suggest you stop talking to Keeva about her eggs drying up and meeting your mom, and a lot of other heavy shit. She is not in the baby-making, Mama-meeting mode, so stop acting like a cave man. That kind of behavior won't endear Keeva to you, Amos. She has a lot of baggage that started when she was a child and you won't overcome it by urging her to meet your mom. You'll just scare the hell out of her."

Shelley, resuming his role as the Trailblazer's captain decides to take charge of the conversation. "This issue between you and Keeva is not going to be solved overnight, Amos. Let's remember that this is Adaris and Jackie's day and all make the most of it. Just one word of advice to all of you just married, were married, and never been married. If you feel you've gotten stuck, try going back to the beginning and remember what made you like or love your mate so much. And I don't mean just the sex. Think about why you fell for her and then center on that feeling. Tiffany and I have been married for almost three years now, and believe me, I wouldn't trade being married for anything. It is the hardest shit you will ever do and sometimes you feel like you are in hell, but that's outweighed by the euphoria of feeling like you are in heaven—if you have the right mate."

"Clap, clap, clap, clap. That soliloquy deserves a standing ovation. Since Shelley is so full of knowledge, I say we should leave on that note," says World.

As the men start to move down the hall, Amos is thinking about the day he met Keeva and he is smiles . . .

***

I run into the jewelry store and get some fabulous earrings and am back in the hotel with about five minutes to spare.

"Keeva, thanks for getting the earrings. I just pray I can find the ones I lost. Adaris paid a grip for them and I'll feel awful if they don't turn up," says Jackie.

"No sweat, girl. The timing was perfect—all this crying was starting to get on my nerves. Aunt Ella has been crying for the last two weeks."

"And so has Leo, but that's because he thought his supply of free football tickets would dry up now that Adaris has retired. At least until he remembered that Shelley and Chris are still in the league. Being locked up in the pen for three years left Leo with a lot of football to catch up on."

"How about you take his ass back to St. Croix with you when you leave on Monday? I swear he is getting on my last nerve," says Serena with a big sigh. "He calls me at least three times a day to tell me about his classes and the wonderful people he is meeting in school. Between Leo and dealing with Mom over this reception, I have been pulling my hair out."

"I love Leo like a step-brother, but no thanks, chica. What kind of friend would I be to deprive you of Leo and his worrying the hell out of you? And if I brought him to St. Croix about 20 women would fall in love with him. Pretty soon the island would be populated with a whole bunch of mini Leos." Max laughs at her own joke.

"Why are you so quiet over there Keeva? I can't believe you don't have anything to say about Leo getting on your nerves," says Serena, rolling her eyes.

"Amos is worrying me enough to cancel Leo out. Maybe we need to make sure that Amos and Leo hook up so they can worry the hell out of each other," says Keeva with a frown.

"Speaking of worrying, Jackie, word on the street is that your ex point guard Scoop is pissed about the recently wed couple and plans to come to the reception with the rest of the team to give Adaris a piece of his mind for taking his best girl," says Keeva.

"You also need to be on the lookout for your step-son, AJ. I heard he and Peaches had a beef over your statistician, now known as Keeva's intern Sophia," says Rena with a bark of laughter.

"Looks like we got a regular rerun of the *Best Man* movie about to take place. Thank God Peaches and Scoop will be on their way to the military and college in the next few months so they can meet new women to help them get over you and Sophia," says Max.

"Who knew over a year ago that so many relationships would start and end? And thank God, because Jackie, you could have caught a case. Not for getting with a student but for strangling him! Scoop took puppy love to the extreme, didn't he girl?" asks Keeva.

Jackie shakes her head and says, "Yeah, who knew my star point guard would fall for his coach. But that lasted only a few seconds, until I started making his little butt run for talking too damn much."

"Keeva, we all know that you're the master of diversion, but don't think for one second we have forgotten about the secret love affair you and Amos have been having since August. We also know you only hibernate with men in the fall and winter, then break up with them between Christmas and Valentine's Day, but it's starting to get hot outside and . . ." Rena says, prodding her gently.

"You got it twisted, Rena. I wait until after Valentine's Day to break up with them. Who am I to keep some lucky fool from buying me flowers and chocolate on the most expensive day of the year? And just so you know, in order to break up with someone you have to be with him. Amos and I started off wrong. He got on my bad side right off by insinuating that he may have seen me at the club doing my exotic dancer thing. Everyone knows I was just a waitress at that club," says Keeva with a huff.

"Well cousin, turn your frown upside down. I's married now and we are going to party like its 1999. So put on those gold dresses I let you design, and don't forget the purple Manolo Blahniks I so unselfishly bought you and those fierce earrings that my hubby is going to faint over when he gets his AmEx bill next month—especially yours, Keeva. Let's go shake a tail feather!"

# Let the Games Begin

The day I met Keeva I was just minding my own business. Right before our season opener, Adaris asked if I wanted to hang out with him and a few of our team mates and their ladies after the game. Never one to pass on a free meal, I decided to join in. Adaris and I have become pretty tight over the last few years. We both joined the squad at the same time; me as a second round draft pick and Adaris from the Cowboys.

I come from a large military family and an even larger farming family. Most of my folks are from South Georgia and harvested cotton for generations. My grandfather got smart and decided he didn't want to grow cotton the rest of his life, so he decided to join the military. Robbins Air Force Base was about 30 miles from home, and he was stationed there until he was sent to serve in World War II. In my opinion, he jumped from the fat into the frying pan, but I guess it wasn't any worse to take orders from the lieutenant than from the "master."

My grandparents had five children—back in the day that's what people did—and my dad followed in his father's footsteps and joined the Air Force. Although the military took my dad around the world, our family stayed in Macon on my grandparent's farm. We had enough acreage for everyone to have their own parcel of land, close enough to see each other every day but far enough to go to our own piece of land every evening. My family harvested not only cotton but a large crop of vegetables and pecans, and we also had a few cows and horses. Since my family depended on farming to earn a living, I spent most of my time on the farm. But, I decided at a pretty early age that I did not want to be a third-generation military man or a farmer. I wanted to have a career that allowed me to make my own decisions and not be at the beck and call of someone giving me orders all day. Which is of course ironic, since I now play pro football.

I was a large child who became a large teenager. Once I got to junior high, our football coach decided he wanted me to try my hand at football. By my senior year I had grown another five inches and packed on more weight. I was recruited by the University of Georgia and quickly accepted. The military has done some wonderful things for our family, but I have also seen it destroy families, and I decided a career playing football was far better than joining the military. In a sense, football was my savior.

After I made the choice to risk my life as a college football player rather than as an army officer, I felt I had something to prove. That something eventually included a 3.2 GPA, the Rimington Trophy Award, the Jacobs Blocking Award, and several UGA records. I also kept my nose clean.

Anyhow, I was rocking along in Nashville, minding my own business, until I walked into the hotel suite and cast my eyes on Keeva. I had never seen such beauty in such a tiny package. I can only describe her as five feet of fire! I was drawn to her like a moth to a flame. She is not only beautiful, she has a personality to match, and her heart is so big. At first I was just wasting a little time by flirting and getting to know her. It was the beginning of football season and I knew that as a newbie I needed to concentrate on the season ahead. But something about Keeva kept me coming back for more . . . more punishment as it turns out. I don't know what her ex-husband did to her, but that girl is angry! And that anger is often directed at me. Now don't get me wrong, a little assertiveness can be a good thing but, she is always on ten!

Over the last few months Keeva has allowed me to take her out to dinner and visit her at home, but I'm getting tired of being used as a booty call. I honestly feel like the roles are reversed in this relationship, as Keeva calls all the shots. She tells me when I can see her, where I can see her, and sometimes she won't even answer my calls! And then when I leave a message she has the nerve to text, "What's up?" Now think about that. She is just like a dude. When she decides to grant me some of her time I have to drop everything, because who knows when she'll let me see her again. Now I see how women get so obsessed with men. Keeva just keeps me guessing. Sometimes she is so sweet that she makes my toes curl. Other times I could just choke her.

After months of going back and forth with Keeva and feeling like the dude on *Boomerang* after Robin Givens left the money on the bedside table, I have decided enough is enough! My little heart can take getting put off just so many times. I am young, single, smart, good looking, athletic, and reasonably wealthy. I have all my teeth, which is unusual for a country boy, and I love my Mama. What more could she want? I know I am a little bit younger than Keeva, which would technically make her a cougar, and I am Ok with that, but my Mama didn't raise no fool, and I have decided to put my size 15 foot down today and let Keeva know what's up. I decided to invite a buddy of mine named Jazzmine to escort me to the reception, just to shake things up a bit!

***

I know this is not a good time to reflect, right when I'm about to be an almost bridesmaid and all, but I can't help thinking back to the day I met Amos. I had no business taking my ass to that game—I knew it would turn out crazy because Jackie and Adaris were not in a good place. Well, in an awkward place, because Adaris decided to put things on hold when he found out that Jackie was coaching his son. He didn't want her or his son to have the added issue of the coach also being his dad's girlfriend.

When Chris saw that the Giants were playing Adaris' team, he thought it would be great for Max to come to Tennessee and kill two birds with one stone. She could spend some time with Jackie and see him play. That was a great idea in theory, but in reality it sucked. You see, Adaris had also invited several other women to the game and they all ended up in the owner's suite. Not all spread out across a stadium that seats 50,000 people, but in a room designed to hold 50. Adaris is charming but sometimes not very smart.

After the game, Adaris was trying to make peace with Jackie, so he invited some of the guests up to his hotel room to have dinner. That included Jackie and her girls—and yes, yours truly. I had no idea what to expect, but I certainly didn't expect to meet the "bone crusher." When that hotel door opened, four of the finest men I had seen in the entire US of A—*and I do mean finest*—came sauntering into the room, all booted and suited and smelling like spring rain with a hint of musk. Those four would have made any red-blooded woman stop and stare, but after I came out of my trance I realized that three of the men were taken. Well, Chris and Shelley were taken, and Adaris was about to get his ass whooped. But then I looked up, and believe me I had to look waaay up, I saw this massive guy with the complexion of a Hershey dark chocolate bar, feet the size of a boat, hands bigger than a catcher's mitt, and, well, everything about him was just huge!

He also was very handsome, and I could tell by the sparkle in his eye that he wasn't Santa Claus. He sauntered over to me, stuck out that big ole hand, and said "Hello" in the "countriest" voice I had heard in a long time—and that's saying something since I live in the heart of Tennessee. He muttered something about being a growing boy and I should come over and sit by him. By the end of dinner he had invited himself for a ride in my damn limo and offered to make it rain, but he also made me laugh more than any other man in a long time. He was like a breath of fresh air—the kind of air that you knew was not running any games, was a load of fun, and had a heart of gold.

So what is wrong with Amos? Absolutely nothing, which is what scares the hell out of me! He is damn near perfect, except for his size—everything is big, if you get my drift—but for someone so large he sure knows how to move. He doesn't have an ounce of fat on him and is constantly monitoring what I put in my mouth—says he wants me to get healthier so my body will be ready when we start to have children! Whoa! I am not ready to have any big babies or even get married. I'm still hurting about being cheated on and lied to, and although I'm learning to trust Amos, it's only as far as I can throw him— about an inch!

My shrink constantly reminds me that I have trust issues. Can you believe I pay that heifer $100 an hour to tell me that crap? I am a firm believer that the only reason people go to counseling is to verify things they already know. Let's see . . . she has already confirmed the fact that I am bossy, an overachiever, have Napoleon syndrome, have trust issues, commitment issues, and am materialistic (but only when I'm under extreme stress). On the other hand, I am honest to a fault, loyal to my family, and very emotional. Some of those characteristics have served me extremely well in my career, but they have ruined me in terms of having a good relationship.

Believe me, Amos should be glad I'm not ready if he'd just think about it. If I did settle down with him I'd be an overbearing, bossy, possessive wife who would kick any woman's ass for coming anywhere near him . . . in a loving way, of course. I know that sounds like all kinds of crazy, but I'm just saying that I am saving the boy a lot of heartache. Not to mention that I am several years older than Amos. All I will say is he is in his mid-twenties and I am in my early thirties. I know I look good for my age, but what happens when Amos sees a younger woman who isn't fighting gravity as hard as I will be ten years from now?

But the person who said that the worse you treat people the more they come after you was a genius. I treat Amos like hell most of the time, but he just keeps coming back for more punishment. I even pulled out the old dating handbook and

27

have tried pretty much every move in it. Rule #1, don't talk on the phone too much. They become too attached. Rule #2, never let them spend the night at your house. They become too attached. Rule #3, never go over to their house. Rule #4, don't get to know their family, especially their mom. Rule #5, don't cook for them—that one's easy, because I can't cook worth a damn! But the rules didn't work. The meaner I was to Amos, the sweeter he was to me. Wining and dining me. Cooking for me at my own house. Sending me flowers at work. Leaving little notes here and there. He even watched chick flicks with me! The harder I tried, the harder he tried, and it was working. Well, it was until I came to my senses.

I decided last week that enough is enough. I have spent more time with Amos in the last few months than I have with any man in the last few years. I was starting to settle into his big ole warm arms, and I can't have that. It is time for Amos Hunter and me to have the talk. After this reception I am going to let him have it!

***

Ella eyes her daughter and sniffs, "Oh Jackie baby, you look just beautiful! I am so glad you let Rena, Keeva, and I have a reception for you here at home."

Jackie looks around the room at Max, Keeva, Serena, and Ella. "It would have been a beat down if Adaris and I didn't renew our vows in front of our families. I hope you all can

28

forgive me—we had waited so long to be together that we just couldn't wait any longer."

"Who can stay mad at you, especially with you looking so beautiful in that purple dress. Anyone else as tall as you would look like Barney, but you just look lovely," says Max.

"I agree with you there. Who knew that a dark purple dupioni silk would look so gorgeous? But I must admit that the gold dresses Gail made for all of us are just smashing. I can't wait to see the look in Amos' eyes when he sees me in this," says Keeva.

Rena frowns at Keeva. "Wait a minute—I thought you were breaking up with Amos today? Only you would pick such a joyous time to break someone's heart."

"Shut up Rena! I am not breaking his heart. Amos knew the rules of the game when we started. Nothing serious, just fun."

"Well, dude, looks like a lady to me! You know you like that boy. When you talk about him you get this funny look on your face. If it weren't you, I would swear it's a smile," Jackie says. "Why don't you stop acting so hard, Keev. The people who know you best are in this very room, and we can read you like a book. Why don't you just admit how much you like Amos and put him and all of us out of our misery?"

"I concur with Jackie," Max says. "So what if you're a few years older and that you look like a china doll next to Amos? You look really cute together, and maybe between the two of you, you can have some average size kids," she adds with a chuckle.

"Careful bitch! I am not the only person with trust issues up in this piece. I bet you are glad that everyone is all over me like a duck on a Junebug so they can leave you alone. Why is it that you keep holding Chris at bay? I have a reason not to trust—what's yours?" Keeva says with a huff.

"Keep in mind that the reason for the season is Jackie, so after I answer your question, we need to focus on getting her out there to renew her vows. Chris and I are working through our issues. I can't just drop a career to run halfway across the world to shack up. Why buy the sheep if you can get the milk for free!" says Max.

"It's why buy the cow if you can get the milk, Max. And I think the topic of Amos and Chris needs to be discussed over a glass of wine when we have about five spare hours," says Jackie.

"As long as we don't let you drink too many glasses that will be fine. The last time you drank Pinot you were off the chain," says Keeva with a laugh.

"What happened the last time you drank Pinot, Jackie? I vaguely remember Keeva mentioning after a football game that you had gotten a little drunk," says Ella with a frown.

"Mom, it's a long story," Serena says. "The good thing is that Jackie's drunken stupor led to a solid understanding between her and Adaris. It also started a little love affair between Amos and Keeva. But enough about that. Let's get lined up so we can march in. I am going to run and get Leo so he can escort you in, Jackie." She rushes out the door.

"This day is bittersweet, ladies," says Jackie. "One of the reasons I agreed to elope is because Daddy isn't here to walk me down the aisle. But his two little mini-me's, Leo and Jordan, will be close by." Jackie's eyes are teary as she follows Keeva, Max, and Ella out the door.

# Running Away

Adaris and Jackie decided to renew their vows at the beautiful Hutton Hotel, the place where a lot of this relationship foolishness started. By his third date with Jackie, Adaris said God had revealed to him that Jackie would be his wife. Unbeknownst to Jackie, Adaris began to build a dream house for the two of them—and their future children. He had been living with his mother, but also had a room at the Hutton so he could stay near the stadium on days when it was difficult to get home, particularly after a game. Needless to say, Jackie and Adaris created some wonderful, and some not so wonderful, memories at this place. This is also where I set my eyes on Amos for the first time, so memories are running like bad kids through the corridor of my mind.

Rena and I have managed to make purple and gold look really beautiful together. I guess we pulled it off by adding a little cream to soften the purple. The music starts and I begin to walk down the aisle, and I finally take a deep breath. All of our hard work has paid off and many dreams are being fulfilled on this day.

Of course, since I'm the shortest I'm the first one down the aisle. I was pissed about it and griped about why the first should be last, but Jackie shut me up quickly by saying the guys were going in reverse order, since Amos was the largest. I stomped off in a huff thinking, who told you to line that big ass chump up with me anyway! Why not line me up with Micah, Chris, or Shelly? And then reality set in. I am pretty sure Rena, Max, and Tiffany would not approve of me in all my loveliness being escorted by their husbands and significant others, so I shut up pretty quick. Who am I kidding? I'm by far the prettiest in the bunch, and who doesn't want to hear the crowd gasp when the bridal party first walks in? Truth be told, those four heifers can hold their own in the looks department any day. We are all traffic stoppers!

To keep us from whining, Jackie let us bridesmaids design our own dresses. Over the years I have learned to compensate for my slight stature by emphasizing my better body parts. In my humble opinion—and that of about 95% of the men I have dated—I have pretty sensational legs, and when you put me in 3-inch heels it makes my gams look smashing. With that in mind, I chose a simple dress with a halter at the top that flows into a straight pencil skirt that's a little longer in the back. I decided not to wear Spanx or panty hose and to just let it all hang out. Thanks to my thrice weekly workouts I'm looking pretty tight and right, and feel comfortable leaving all things ungirdled and ungathered. I made sure to rub extra Vaseline onto my legs so I am looking bright and shiny. I also decided to wear my hair in a wispy bun to emphasize my big gray eyes— my second best asset.

I walk into the reception hall and do a quick scan to make sure everything is in place. The bad thing about Rena and me planning this reception is that we have to rely on our assistants to handle everything today. We're both control freaks, so relinquishing control over something this important is difficult. Kyle, Rena's assistant, and Sophia, Jackie's statistician, are working as our free slave—I mean assistants— and appear to be doing a smashing job. The guests have actually arrived on time, which is saying something for black folks. I guess they got the hint on the invitation that said, "Reception hall doors will close promptly at 5:55 pm." In layman's terms, if you don't get your ass in here by that time, you won't get in. Period.

The Stevie Wonder song *A Ribbon in the Sky* starts to play, and it's time for me to make my grand entrance. I look toward the front of the room and see the guys standing under a trellis of purple and ivory roses, but my eyes narrow in on Amos. I haven't seen him in a suit since last September, and what a sight he is. All the men are wearing beautiful cream suits with purple bow ties, and each tie has a different pattern. As I stare into Amos' eyes I can tell that he is impressed. His eyes travel from the top of my head to my size 5 Blahniks, then back up again, and he gives me the sweetest smile. I start to grin back at him when I see his eyes shift to his left. Then I see him smiling at someone in the audience. What the hell—that smile

34

is meant only for me, dammit! Ok, Keeva, keep your composure. Don't let him see you sweat! Put your sexy walk on just in case there are other interested parties out there and just keep walking.

Maybe he was smiling at his mom. But wouldn't he have told me if she was coming? Maybe it's one of his teammates? No, that was definitely a smile meant for a woman. I have got to calm myself down so I don't run down this aisle and smack the shit out of him. Ok, Keeva, snap out of it. You can't trick the tricker. You can't play the player. You can't fool the . . . wait a minute! Has Amos been playing me for a fool this whole time, making me think he's ready to settle down and have babies? I feel a red glaze start to pass over my eyes, then suddenly remember some sage advice Uncle Shorty once gave me: "You can show him better than you can tell him." So, I decide to show Amos a thing or two . . . at least I plan to once this vow renewal is done.

***

Jazzmine, the best seamstress in Nashville made the groomsmen's suits. That girl measures you from the rooter to the tooter, and I must admit I've never had clothes that fit me so well. My fittings usually take a long time, so we have really gotten to know each other. She is the Mindy to my Mork, Lucy to my Charlie Brown, and Angel to my Charlie. We are down like two flat tires. She is a great listener and has given me some great advice about dealing with women.

I must admit, Amos is looking pretty good and his tie is banging. I wasn't sure how this off-white suit would look on a big guy like myself, but by the fourth fitting Jazzmine had convinced me that ecru is a great color for my skin.

I was looking forward to hanging out with Jazz at the reception. She meets my three requirements—tall, thick, and tantalizing—which I broke when I met Keeva.

I haven't seen Keeva in over a week. She refused to see me before the wedding so I couldn't get a feel where her head is at today. I wanted to warn her that I brought a date to the reception. Well, I didn't actually bring Jazz with me. She came on her own to do some last minute alterations, but I did plan to hang out with her tonight. Jazz is drama free and easy to be with. She doesn't judge me or make me feel guilty about enjoying her company.

When Keeva walks through the door I almost keel over. Who in the hell allowed her to wear that dress! She looks tall, thick, and—oh damn she meets all of my requirements! Her hair is up and she is looking soft. I have to look away to keep myself from charging up the aisle to grab her. I turn and look at Jazz so she can get me back on track. It didn't help. Amos is officially a goner. As Keeva gets closer I start to smell her, which really gets me going. I have got to do something to stay in control. Thank God Max is on her way down the aisle. Maybe I can focus on someone else for a few minutes.

***

We walk down the aisle and then wait as Leo leads Jackie down the aisle to Luther Vandross' *So Amazing.* The love is shining in Adaris' and Jackie's eyes, sending a chill down my spine. I steal a look at Amos and see that familiar twinkle in his eye, but then I remember he shared my twinkle with some other star a mere minute ago, so I roll my eyes and turn back to the loving couple. As they repeat their vows there is not a dry eye in the room. The ceremony is absolutely beautiful.

"What's wrong with you chica? You can cut the tension with a sword," Max whispers to me as we gather to take pictures.

"It's cut the tension with a knife, Max. And I am not going to let him ruin my day!"

"Last time I checked this was Adaris and Jackie's day, and who the hell are you talking about?" says Max looking around the room.

"Who do you think I'm talking about, Max?" I whisper while crumpling my flowers.

"Stop ruining your flowers, Keeva. I assume you're talking about Amos if you weren't so deep in denial."

"I swear I saw him looking out into the audience a few minutes ago smiling at someone!"

"Since we have no idea who that could be in this roomful of 350 people, I suggest you let the mystery unfold. You of all people should know how to spot an intruder. Don't you remember the detective work we did for Jackie a few months ago?"

"That's where all this shit started, Max! And did you just say 350 people? I better go find Kyle. It looks like we are going to need more seating for the 50 people who didn't RSVP, the bastards!"

"You may want to wait till we finish taking these pictures. The photographer is waving us over now. And you, my pretty, are about to be wedged right in between Amos and Shelley."

"Any other day I would be ecstatic to be sandwiched between two hot, rich men, but I am not in the mood today. And Shelley is married. Do you think Jackie will miss me if I disappear for a minute?"

"Of course she will, stupid! I thought you were the player from Asia. Get your butt over there and show Amos what you are working with. That is, if he hasn't punked you out," Max says with a smile.

"I swear, Max, I wish you would stop trying to use all these stupid colloquialisms! It's the playa from the Himalaya, you dummy! And I ain't nobody's punk," I say, stomping away.

"Tell that to the flowers you just demolished. I hope Jackie throws you her bouquet so you can replace the ones you just ruined!" Max says with a screech of laughter.

***

"Ok wedding party. I'm going to line up the entire group in just a minute, but the bride and groom also want pictures of all of you paired up. So, let's see . . . Amos and Keeva, I need you up here first."

I am going to kill Jackie for taking all these damn pictures today. But if I think about it, we are the people closest in the world to the newly re-wed couple. Why wouldn't she want to take pictures! I just don't want to stand so close to Amos, with him looking all good and smelling all good and him smiling at me. I am not in the mood for it, especially after that little smile he gave who knows who! I'm supposed to be breaking up with him today anyway. Break up with him . . . I must be delusional—how can you break up if you were never together! As I sashay over to stand in the embrace of my soon-to-be broken up lover, I start to feel a little mushy. I give myself a shake to get it together.

"Keeva, you are looking beautiful today. I wish you didn't wear that dress so short. Your milkshake is bringing all the boys to the yard, including your boy Amos," Amos says with a leer.

"Ok, big guy, I am going to move you a little closer to this beautiful young lady. Move your arm so that it rests right up against her stomach, just like so." The photographer moves Amos' arm across my belly.

"That's perfect," Amos says. He moves as close as he can so his torso is resting right up against my back.

"Amos, don't push up on me too close. I don't want you to get too excited."

Amos leans down and whispers, "Baby girl, it looks like you are the excited one. I can tell just by looking at the pulse in your neck. I also noticed that your breathing just changed. Amos has got skills, if you know what I mean."

"My pulse is beating fast because I just ran from the back of the room."

Amos leans further down and places a tender kiss on my neck, then tightens his arm around my stomach to keep me from falling. "Well, I hope you catch your breath soon darling, 'cause if Amos can get you by just a kiss, I can't wait to see what would happen if I did this." He tightens his hand against my stomach while gently running his fingers down my arm.

"Maam, are you ok? You look like you just got a little light-headed. Lean your head back and tilt it a little to the left, and then smile for me," says the photographer.

"Yeah baby, tilt that butt a little more to the left. That's it right there," Amos whispers as he smiles into the lens.

"You big freak! I can't believe you are accosting me in front of all of these people. And stop rubbing against me!"

"You know you like it, Keeva. And if you had answered my calls this week you could have had more of Amos."

"I was too busy running around to get ready for this shindig. I didn't have time to talk."

"Didn't have time or didn't have the desire? We need to talk about our future, Keeva. Now smile for the photographer one last time, and tell me we can see each other later this evening or early tomorrow," says Amos, still rubbing my arm as he smiles into the lens.

"I am not going to make a booty call tonight, Amos!"

"I never asked you to make a booty call, Keeva. That was your decision, not mine. I actually have better morals than you give me credit for. In fact, there is a lot you don't know about Amos. Now smile really big so we can get this over with, or I may put a move on you that will make you pass out."

"You wish you could put it down like that," I say through gritted teeth.

"Amos has just begun, but if you don't get yourself together you may just miss out."

"And give the bitch you were smiling at a few minutes ago a chance to squirm her way in."

"Keeva, you are too beautiful to have a potty mouth like that. What did I tell you about expressing yourself without cussing," Amos says, giving me a little tap on my stomach.

"You ain't running nothing up in here but your mouth. Ok, the photographer is done, so your big bone crushing ass can let me go now!"

"This little talk is not over. Go ahead and have a tantrum like you always do when you don't get your way, teeny tiny. I like it when you get riled up." Amos gently pushes me away and turns to talk to Chris, who is on his way to the stage.

Oh no, he didn't just get me hot under the collar, call me teeny tiny, and then dismiss me! I must be off my game to let him get away with that crap. Just wait until we talk later. I am going to get him. But I must admit that young, big tenderoni had me going for a minute. I mentally shake myself and return to wedding coordinator mode. At our next encounter I am going to cut him off at the knees.

***

Keeva just stomped away from me, pouting. If she hadn't, there is no telling what I would have done. I have missed that girl something fierce this last week, and I almost blew it. I am not into game playing, but I am certainly not into being played either. It's time for me to give little Miss Hudson-McGhee some of her own medicine, and if it means a sensual seduction, I am all for it. Thank God she hasn't realized that I smiled at Jazz during the ceremony. The cat will soon be out of the bag, and once that bomb drops I am going to have to stay as close to Jazz as possible to keep Keeva from killing her. Or maybe Jazz will need to stay close to me to prevent my demise. Either way, it's about to get exciting in here. My boy Adaris can't have all the excitement today. We groomsmen need to have some fun as well. And why should I let this ecru suit go to waste? Keeva is about to learn that I am a young buck and that I can keep up with her. In fact I plan to stay at least three steps ahead of her and outwit her. My immature behavior is either going to work like a charm or backfire right in my face!

***

"Jackie, I hate to barge in on you while you are changing clothes, but I need to take a break girl."

"Max had the same idea—she just went into the bathroom. Why aren't you downstairs enjoying the reception, girl? I heard the hors d'oeuvres are being passed out and people are starting to loosen up. I told Adaris not to have an open bar. You know your people like a free drink," Jackie says while pulling her dress over her head. "Thank God you and Rena came up with the idea of drink tickets so people don't go too far."

"We came up with the three ticket limit to keep our drunk ass family members from embarrassing us. Bo just asked me a few minutes ago if we were having a raffle with the tickets."

"And what did you tell him, cuz?"

"I told him to hang on to the tickets until the end of the night because we are having a drawing for a 60-inch plasma HD TV," Keeva says with a laugh.

"You didn't! You know Bo is not going to stop pestering Rena about that TV all night. He's your brother. Why do you want to make him look like a fool?"

"Because he is one. I don't know how in the hell we had the same mother but turned out so differently. Oh yeah, I know, we have different fathers. And you know Uncle Shorty says you can't fix stupid."

"So why are you in here? I saw you and Amos getting cozy during the pictures a few minutes ago. You look like a china doll in his arms."

"That's precisely the reason I'm in here. I'm going to break up with Amos tonight and I need to get my head together before we have 'the talk.'"

"Break up! Since when are the two of you a couple? The last time we discussed your relationship with Amos you adamantly said that you were just friends," says Jackie.

"Well, we are just friends but he wants more and I don't."

"Then why don't you stop stringing the poor boy along?" Max asks as she walks in the room.

"What are you doing in here, Max? The last time I saw you, you and Chris were hugged up. You taking a breather?" says Keeva.

"Don't hate girl. My boo and I are doing just fine," says Max, rolling her eyes.

"Fine, as long as he follows your damn rules, Max. You do know he will get tired of the long distance romance sooner or later. Then what?"

"Stop throwing pepper, Keeva. If I was in the same city like you and Amos I wouldn't have the same insecurities. You can run but you can't hide," says Max with a snide smile.

"Ladies, ladies. This day is all about me. So stop throwing salt, Max. Let's go back out there before Rena sends the Calvary after us." Jackie hooks arms with Keeva and Max as they walk out the door.

## Third Wheel

As we walk back into the reception hall, I can tell most people have reached their three drink ticket limit and are three sheets to the wind. The noise is deafening—it's as if everyone in the room is trying to talk above the band, and the louder they get, the louder the band gets. Adaris is not much of a dancer, but Jackie has convinced him to do the first dance together, especially since her dad isn't there. Adaris walks Jackie out onto the dance floor as Rena introduces them to the guests—who obviously already know who they are. They take their first steps to the tune of Stevie Wonder's *You and I.*

As the music plays, I scan the room to see if I can get a glimpse of Amos. I don't see him, but I know he is around somewhere—there is no way his big ass is going to miss any free food. Just when every woman in the room (and even some of the men) start to tear up watching the happy couple, who are so clearly deep in love, the music shifts to a fast tune that sounds like EU's *Doing the Butt,* and Jackie starts backing it up in Adaris' face. I am shocked! Jackie is one of the most conservative people I know. I realize this song reminds them of a time they unexpectedly met up at a high school dance they both were chaperoning—a few things happened under the bleachers that night and it sealed their love. I spot Aunt

Ella in the crowd and she looks aghast! This dance was obviously a well-kept secret.

*Doing the Butt* sparks an upbeat mood and other couples join the newlyweds on the dance floor. Just as I turn to find Amos so I can show him a little of my own rump, I see him out there already dancing! Who is that rubbing her derriere up against him? It's Jazzmine. With two Zs. Haberdasher to the stars. She has her tail feather all up on my boo's private parts, and I don't like it one bit!

I take a deep breath and tell myself, Keeva girl, you can't let him see you lose all of your cool points. You can't be acting one minute like you don't want the boy and the next get pissed off because he's humping the haberdasher. So I do what any real woman would do. I grab the closest man and drag him onto the dance floor. As I am dragging said man I realize he's really just a boy, AJ's baby brother, Noah. The biggest problem is that he's 15 years old and the little creep has been after me since the opening game of the last football season. In light of Noah's age, I figure I better keep our dance rated PG. Dammit, why didn't I grab Adaris' Uncle Cleeve—we could at least have done the funky chicken. As I'm dancing with a real-life boy toy, I keep peeking over at Amos and the "Dasher," which will henceforth be her moniker. I'm devastated to see they are having a blast.

I realize there are only two emotions a bridesmaid can have at times like this: abject misery or blissful fun. Just as Noah and I move into the stinky leg, the DJ puts on a slow song. Noah is taller—a lot taller—than my five feet, and he looks down at me, then holds out his hand as if I will want to join him in a slow grind. I not so regretfully decline and walk off the floor to find someone more age appropriate. I glance slyly to my left and see that Amos and Dasher have not left the dance floor. In fact, he has gathered her closer and they're now slow dancing and talking. I can hardly keep myself from stomping over to break up their little *tête-à-tête*, and I figure this is a good time to run to the ladies room. As I head that way, I try to figure out how I'm going to get my too tight dress over my hips or below my knees. That's what I get for asking Gail to tighten it last week. I'm not a fan of public restrooms, so I go to the room reserved for the wedding party. As I walk through the door I literally run into Max's 42DDSs.

"Max, every time I turn around you're coming out of the bathroom. If I didn't know better I'd think you have irregular bowel syndrome."

"Very funny, Keeva. I don't know what it is, but I have been peeing a lot lately."

"Well, you may want to see your doctor when you get back home because it could also be diabetes or a bladder infection. Or you could be preg—"

Before I can finish the sentence, Max is on me like white on rice. She throws her hand, three- inch red nails and all, over my mouth so quickly that I stumble. We tussle for a few seconds and I finally pull her hand from my face. I back up a few steps, put my hands on my hips, and whisper, "Attorney, Doctor Maxine Isadora Hilton, are you with child?"

"Shut up Keeva! At this point I don't know what I am with. But it ain't helping with you monitoring all of my bathroom breaks!"

I move as close as Max's bodacious tatas will allow, and then begin to fire questions at her.

"When was your last period Max?"

"About four weeks ago."

"Are you usually regular?"

With a huff Max whispers, "I have been regular my entire life."

"Are you nauseated?"

"The word is nauseous and I feel fine."

"Don't get smart girly. Are you and Chris practicing safe sex?"

"Keeva, you are not my mother, so stop asking so many damn questions and back up a few feet, you're making me nervous."

I grab Max's hands and say, "Answer me Max!"

"Yes, we are having safe sex. I insisted on it, especially since Chris is my first . . ."

Now, when Max says that, I drop her hands, step back, and start pacing. And then I yell, "Your first! How in the hell can a 30-year-old woman go that long without having sex?"

Max throws her hands around my neck and says, "Shut your pie crack! Only three people know that; my mom, Jackie, and Chris. And now you. Yes, I was a virgin before Chris, 'cause I didn't want to sleep with just anyone. And yes, Chris most certainly rocked my world!"

"It's pie hole, Max. Did you get on the pill once you started?"

"I thought about it, but since Chris and I aren't together every day I thought the prophylactics would work."

"Nobody says prophylactics, Max! It's rubber, or condom, or—well, never mind that. Your smart ass should know that they are not fail proof!"

"I'm only a few days late so there is no need to get your panties in the water at this point. So let's pretend we didn't have this little conversation and get back to the reception."

"It's get your panties in a wad, and I don't have any on under this dress. I would strongly suggest you pick up a pregnancy test, and soon, so you can confirm whether or not I'm going to be a godmother. And yes, I have first dibs since

I'm the one who made this little discovery. Now move, I need to pee myself and go back to watching Amos and Dasher."

"Who is Dasher?"

"Never mind, girl. You got bigger fish to fry. Speaking of which, now I know why Aunt D dreamed about fish a few days ago. She has been blowing up Serena's and Jackie's and my phone asking if we're pregnant."

"Keeva, please don't say anything to anybody. It could just be my nerves. Chris has been putting a lot of pressure on me to take the next step in our relationship."

"So why the hesitation, Max? You know he's crazy about you. He is single with no kids . . . at least not yet. He's successful and great looking and he seems to know what he wants."

"I know he's crazy about me and I feel the same way, but things have moved so fast in the last year. We both have a lot of baggage, and I would have to completely change my lifestyle to accommodate him."

"If you want to know about warp speed, just look at Jackie and Adaris. Who knew that her holding out for over a year would lead to a proposal, a big ass house and ring, and a short courtship followed by this party. Not to mention some fabulous earrings. But you're right, this isn't a conversation for today. Right now I need a cocktail and you need some cranberry juice—for now I'm going to jump on the denial train with you and act like you have a bladder infection, but let's talk again tomorrow. I have a feeling this will be one of several hot topics we have to cover."

"Keeva, promise me you won't say anything to Jackie and Rena until I can sort this out."

"I promise girl. But I will make sure I let Aunt D know that I ain't the one with the bun in the oven," I say as I head to the bathroom.

"You off-island African Americans say the dumbest things. Bun in the oven," Max says, looking worried once again.

After this episode with Max, I am drained. It's bad enough watching Amos have so much fun dancing with another woman, but it's even worse seeing Max so confused and upset. My huge boy toy issues are nothing in comparison to what Max and Chris may be dealing with in about 9 months.

The reception is going well. By the time I return from my bio break, Rena is herding our sorority members out to the dance floor to serenade Jackie with the AKA hymn. I absolutely hate this. Usually I leave a reception well before this kind of stuff begins so I don't have to pretend to be excited about singing this boring ass song that nobody but our sorority sisters has ever heard of. Don't get me wrong, I love my sisters. Well, at least I love Rena, Jackie, Max, and a few others. But just the thought of singing that song at any sorority function makes me cringe. Anyhow, we sing the *We*

*Help Each Other* crap, and then Jackie throws her bouquet, which Max catches. Then Adaris tosses the garter, which is caught by a man standing a little too close to Aunt Ella and of course it makes Ella do a whole lot of stammering and blushing.

After that, Rena drags me off to put the wedding gifts in the car that all the cheap mothers brought for Adaris and Jackie after they explicitly stated on the invitation that they would prefer people make donations to the American Cancer Society in honor of Jackie's deceased father my Uncle Shorty and their son AJ who is a Leukemia survivor. By the time I get back, Amos and Dasher are gone. As I look around the room, I suddenly feel deflated. A beautiful day has turned into a sad evening—once again I am alone. For the past few years I've been alone, but never really lonely. I found contentment in being by myself. But the last few hours have shown me that I'm not as immune to the charms of Amos Hunter as I pretend to be.

Three glasses of Moscato and several phone calls to Amos later—the calls went straight to his voicemail—I am on pins and needles. I swear I haven't felt this desperate since I was a junior in high school and my boyfriend wasn't answering his phone. None of the girls or my shrink is available to talk me off the ledge, so I do what any irrationally paranoid and desperate person would do. I get behind the wheel of my car, slightly inebriated, and start driving across Nashville to confront Amos. My common sense isn't totally on hiatus, because I decide to take the back roads instead of the interstate. I figure my chances of killing my fool self or anyone else are much smaller on the side streets. I did say irrational, right? As I head over to Amos' house, dialing his phone number on my hands free because I am determined to be a safe drunk which is an oxymoron. I mainly want to know why Amos is spending time with Jazzmine and why he isn't taking my calls, in that order.

A funny thing happens as I start pounding on Amos' door. I suddenly get sober—and a conscience. What the hell am I doing knocking at his door at 2:00 in the morning? Why am I embarrassing myself by reverting to my desperate high school behavior? Why do I care how Amos feels about me? My now sober self returns to reality and decides I may just have time to run back to my car and leave before he answers the door. I turn around to run down the three steps leading up to Amos' front door, but too late I realize there are four steps. I miss the last one and fall flat on my face. The only thing I can conjure up is thank God I only feel about half the hurt to my arm that I will feel tomorrow. By the time I start to yell with pain the door behind me opens and I see Amos in the light on the porch.

***

The reception was amazing. It's just beautiful to see the love that resonates between my boy Adaris and Jackie. I know this joining was a long time coming. In fact, a few months ago I wasn't sure it would ever happen. Adaris was so miserable in his self-inflicted exile from Jackie during the time she was coaching his son. Thank God common sense prevailed and they've finally started a new life together.

Keeva looked great today. It was really difficult seeing her so close by. I'm thankful that Jazzmine decided to stay at the reception. She helped keep me occupied, and she's also a great dancer and fun companion.

I told Keeva months ago what my intentions are regarding our relationship. That seems to have scared the hell out of her, as she more or less ran for her life. Since our last conversation, Keeva has limited our contact to texting, which makes me feel like I'm in high school again. I am too old for this shit, and I've decided to put my foot down. I know what I want and I am not willing to let Keeva dumb down our relationship. Or me. I pulled out my mack daddy vibe for this girl. I let go of all my cool points and cooked for her, wrote her love letters, and just when I was ready to bring my mother in to meet her, she decides to flip the script.

I may be from the country, but I ain't slow. There are a lot of things Keeva doesn't know about me, and before I head home for a break before football camp starts, she and I are going to have a conversation that will make her decide whether to shit or get off the pot. I finish packing for my trip home and decide to take a shower before I hit the sack. As I step out of the shower, I hear someone beating on my front door. Why don't they just ring the damn doorbell? I take my time toweling off because I figure whoever is dumb enough to beat on my door at 2:00 in the morning is also dumb enough to get a beat down. I throw on a robe and head to the door.

*\*\**

When I see Amos' shadow, I run my tongue around in my mouth to make sure I still have all 28 teeth. It feels like they're all there, and I breathe a big sigh of relief. At least I only have hurt my arm and won't further humiliate myself by being a snaggle tooth. I slowly turn my head around and look up. Amos is wearing only a big black robe, which makes my heart rate speed up. How in the hell am I supposed to catch him with the Dasher and confront him when he is looking that damn good?

*\*\**

I walk to the door and swing it open with the intention to intimidate whoever is on the other side, but I am shocked at what I see. Lying at the bottom of my steps in an impossibly awkward position is Keeva! I don't know if she has passed out or might even be dead, and my heart stops. I quickly run down the steps and snatch her up off the sidewalk.

***

As I take in the magnificence I know lies under Amos' robe, he suddenly bounds down the stairs and picks me up. He gathers me close to his chest and I let out a yelp that can be heard for blocks.

"Ouch! Amos, my arm. Watch my arm!"

"Keeva, what the hell are you doing lying in front of my house? And are you all right?" Amos is clearly worried as he carries me into his house I get a whiff of how wonderful he smells and am about to put my head against his chest, when I remember the reason I am here.

"Put me down Amos," I say, pushing with my good arm. "I can walk. And why in the hell did it take you so long to answer the damn door? Is there someone in there with you?"

***

I gently place Keeva on the ground so I can regain my composure. Seeing her there flat on the ground really scared me. Now that I know she is ok I realize we're about to have an argument. It has the potential to get nasty because I am damn near naked and judging by the stench, she is damn near drunk. I also know that arguing with me is where Keeva is most comfortable, and I ain't having it at 2:00 in the morning.

I take a deep breath but keep my arms around Keeva. I whisper a prayer and then look down into two of the prettiest dark gray eyes I've ever seen. Keeva's eyes are usually light gray and only turn dark when she is either turned on or pissed. I cock my head to the side to try to figure out which mood she is in at the moment.

***

"Get your hands off me Amos and stop looking at me like that. And answer my question!"

"First, Keeva, we are not going to argue on my front steps. In fact, we are not going to argue, period. If you come into my house at this hour, you first have to adjust your attitude and your mouth, and then we need to agree that we are going to talk respectfully to each other. Otherwise I'll call you a cab to take your drunk butt home," Amos says, rubbing my arm.

I look away, take a deep breath, and whisper, "Ok, Amos, but will you please answer my question before I embarrass myself again tonight?"

"Keeva, I am here by myself." Amos grabs my good hand and leads me towards the den.

"Are you ok, baby? Looks like you took a pretty nasty fall. Sit down so I can check you out—I'll get my first aid kit."

Amos walks out of the room, and I gingerly sit down on the sofa, lean back, and close my eyes. The reception, the talk with Max, too much wine, and my fear that Amos was entertaining Jazzmine has worn me out. I suddenly feel a warm cloth caressing my face and then antiseptic stinging my injured arm.

"Ouch! Dammit Amos, you could at least warn me before you put that on my arm!"

"Keeva, baby, stop being such a drama queen. While you were resting I checked to make sure you didn't break your arm or any other body parts. I also checked to make sure you have all your teeth. You're lucky you have only a few scratches, you should be ok in a few days."

I look around and notice that I'm now lying on Amos' couch and that he removed my T-shirt to tend to my bruises. "Amos, I know you majored in horticulture, but you are not a doctor. Thanks for checking me out—I think I'm ok."

"I'm far from being a doctor, but farm animals have the same body parts as humans and I was taught at a young age to care for injured animals. Now, would you like to tell me why you were pounding on my door at 2:00?"

I sit up so I can get close to eye level with Amos and then realize I am much too close. Even though the scent has been out of style for years, Amos can make Drakkar Noir smell so heavenly. I start to lean closer to get another whiff, but then I remember I'm supposed to be pissed.

"I came over because you wouldn't answer your phone, Amos," I say, pushing at his chest with my good hand.

"Stop pushing me, Keeva. I told you violence and yelling don't solve anything except on the gridiron. We are not going to be disrespectful to each other, at least not on my turf. Now,

I didn't answer my phone because my battery died. When I got home I started packing and forgot to turn it back on."

I don't know how his big ass does it, but he has a way of diffusing my anger, and it pisses me off all over again. I look down, trying to gather my thoughts, which is a bad idea because I see his big thigh sticking out from under the too small robe. I take a huge gulp of air and try to regain my composure, then look back up and see Amos smiling down at me with a twinkle in his eye. I say, "Well, I only called to see if you made it home safely. I was concerned about you when you didn't say bye to me before you left the reception."

"So, Keeva, after a week of ignoring my phone calls, answering me with curt texts, and trying to ignore me when you see me having fun with someone else at the reception, you make the assumption that I am avoiding you. Does that sound right?"

I manage to look appalled and then say, "Actually Amos, you got it wrong. I didn't even notice that you were with Jazzmine at the reception, and I only called to wish you a safe trip," I say with the straightest face I can.

I start counting down. Five, four, three, two—then I jump in my seat as Amos lets out a roar of laughter.

"Keeva, you are the worst liar! The main thing I admire about you is your brutal honesty, so don't start lying to me now, ok? If you didn't see me with Jazzmine, how did you know we were together? I also just plugged in my phone and saw eight missed calls from you in a two-hour time span. If you'd left a message I would have called you back. I know you pretty well, baby."

"Ok, Amos. You got me. I know I've been acting like an ass the last few weeks. And I want to apologize for my behavior. You are just so damn all-consuming. You're not only big physically but you have big love. The way you treat me is overwhelming and I just don't know how to take it."

"So, Keeva, because you can't handle my so-called 'big love' you start avoiding me and cut off all physical contact?" Amos looks confused. "I am a big boy, Keeva. If you're uncomfortable with our relationship you need to tell me. I am too damn old for this high school shit, and I know you are too."

"You see, that's what I'm talking about! It's bad enough that I'm older than you—you don't have to throw it in my face. And I haven't been avoiding you, I've been busy with Jackie's reception. And Ms. Mary was here last week."

"You are the one who has an issue with your age, not me. And you all finished planning the reception weeks ago. And I don't give a damn about Ms. Mary. She comes every month at least until you start having my babies and I can work around that. Why don't you stop making excuses?"

"Amos, can you please go put some clothes on? I'm not comfortable with you sitting here in your robe."

"I am in my home. You should be glad I put this robe on. I know you find me sexy. It's ok to admit it," Amos says, raising my chin so I have to look into his smiling eyes.

"Ok, you are sexy as hell. And I love the way you smell, even though that cologne is older than you are. I love the fact that you cook for me and leave me little notes. I am amazed that we converse so intelligently even though you were literally raised in a barn. You make me feel so cherished but-"

"But what, Keeva? Would you rather I treat you like a football groupie? Should I only let you come over after midnight for booty calls and flaunt other women in your face?"

"That's what you did tonight, Amos!"

"No Keeva, that's what you do all the time. I didn't do anything but just be me. When you met me you knew I was a country boy from Georgia who is fortunate enough to play pro football. I am a simple man who just happens to be pretty smart and pretty wealthy. Until I met you I was wasting time in strip clubs, casually dating, and honing my craft on the football field. I want a wife and several kids, and I think you and I could build that future together. But I am not down for ghetto love, Keeva."

I was starting to feel a little mushy, until Amos mentioned ghetto love. "What the hell is ghetto love?"

"Ghetto love is that shit that stops and starts. It's down and dirty make-up sex. It's spending time with other people to make your partner jealous. It's volatile and stressful and stupid. It's that 50 shades of whatever stuff that just doesn't last. It's exciting and nerve wracking and just not healthy. It's the kind of love you look back on and are glad it didn't last. I ain't down for that, Keeva. I want the kind of love my parents had, the kind that is patient and enduring. I want what Adaris and Jackie have and what Ms. Ella and your uncle had. And I am not willing to settle just because some idiot hurt you because he was not man enough or mature enough to be your husband. I may be younger than you, Keeva, but I know what I want and I am not willing to settle for less just to make you feel comfortable."

I lean toward Amos, put my arms around his big neck, and whisper in his ear. "But I gave you my pocketbook!"

"And I would take your pocketbook any day, baby, but I don't just want that. I want your heart and your dedication. It doesn't seem like you're ready for that, so I think it would be best for us to spend some time apart so you can decide what you want. You have to decide whether we are going to be together, or whether we will be 'just friends,'" Amos says. Then he kisses me on the cheek.

I heave a deep sigh and look into Amos' eyes. "I am sorry I tried to cheapen our friendship, Amos. That wasn't fair to you. I have a lot of unresolved issues, and until I deal with them I can't even think about moving forward with you or anybody. Thank you for being so honest about what you want," I say, giving him a soft kiss on his lips.

At that moment I think about giving him the old rub, pat, and slide move that Aunt D taught her nieces. I start to rub my hand down his huge thigh, but then his hand is on top of mine, stopping me. He stares into my eyes, kisses my hand, and says, "I heard about that move, Keeva, and as much as I want your pocketbook, purse, Channel or whatever you call it, I am not going to allow you to seduce me. Our future is much more important than two hours of satisfaction. I am leaving in about six hours to head to Georgia. Let's talk when I get back." With that he leans over to help me put my dirty shirt back on, gives me a big hug, and walks me to my car.

I drive home much more sober than when I started out. Although my arm is throbbing, I feel numb. I refuse to think about the consequences I might have to pay for my behavior over the past few weeks—or whether I can get myself together in time to have a future with Amos Hunter. And then I suddenly think, Did Amos just break up with me?

# The Morning After

Much to my surprise, when I get home after my ordeal with Amos, I sleep like a baby. I'm not sure if it's because of the Moscato or the Amos, but whatever the cause, I wake about noon the next day with a start and a lot of pain. At first I sit there smiling, even though every bone in my body is hurting, because I think Amos must be in the bathroom. Then I frown because I realize it's not the pleasant pain that follows a romp in bed but the gut-wrenching "oh damn" of the fall that happened outside Amos' door. After I take a minute to deal with my sore body, I start to fully feel my embarrassment. How in the world could I have drunk all that cheap wine and let myself drive under the influence, only to fall and then jack up my attempt at seduction? Maybe Jackie and I have switched places, 'cause this is more like something stupid she would have done while she and Adaris were pretending to be broken up. I, Keeva Hudson-McGhee, am a lot of things, but I am not a drunk, clumsy floozy!

It's Sunday, and I know if I call my shrink she'll charge me double time just to talk on the darn phone. I decide I need to get one of the girls on the phone. I know Serena always turns her phone off for at least 24 hours after an event, so strike her off the list. Max is probably up to her large tatas with Chris. Now it makes sense why they are so obsessed with each other—Chris is probably making up for a lot of lost time with his 30-year-old virgin. Just thinking about the problems that are sure to result from Max's little secret make my problems seem miniscule. Now Jackie . . . well, she's not really on her honeymoon since she and Adaris got married a while ago, and even so, payback is a mother. That heifer has called me so many times to rescue her and get advice over the last year that she surely can take some time to talk with me in my time of need.

I gingerly get up to wash my face and brush my teeth before calling Jackie, and when I pick up my phone I notice there's a text from Amos. He wants me to know that he made it to Georgia safely and is looking forward to speaking with me when he gets back. So does that mean he doesn't want to talk to me while he is gone? That question joins the avalanche of other questions I need to ask Jackie.

"Hello!"

"I knew you'd be up. What are you and Dair doing this morning?"

"Hey Keeva! We just finished a bike ride. We were both so excited about how well the reception went that we got up early. We're just finishing up lunch. What are you doing?"

"I'm sitting here trying to figure out what happened to the perfectly beautiful, brilliant, sane person that left my body this morning around 1:30 to become the desperate, jealous, idiotic cougar who showed up at Amos' house at about 2:00."

"What you talking 'bout, Willis? I understand the beautiful and brilliant part, but sane? One of the things I love about you is your insaneness, Keeva. Sooo . . . you finally decided you didn't like your man fraternizing with Jazzmine, huh? Adaris and I had a bet on how long it would take you to react."

"So how much was the bet and who won?"

"Well, I can't tell you what we bet because it's something only married folks can talk about, but I won. Adaris said Amos wouldn't make it out of the reception without you pouncing. See, he doesn't know you as well as I do, Keeva."

"So what did you say, Einstein?"

"I told him you were much more subtle than that and that you'd make your move between midnight and 6:00 a.m. so you could have the element of surprise. Going after him at the reception would be way too predictable, and we all know you are unpredictable."

"Thanks Jackie. Next time bet some money so I can have my share. Yes, I showed up, showed out, and then fell on my face. After that I got demoralized and dismissed, in that order."

"Let's see if I can crack that mystery. Sounds like you came ready for a fight, did something stupid to embarrass yourself, then you fell and you all had make-up sex. Then he laid $200 by your pillow and told you to go home!"

"I wish. To make a long story short, I set myself up to catch Jazzmine at Amos' house but had absolutely no plan what to do when I did. After beating on his door for about five minutes I suddenly did a reality check and decided to sneak off. That's when I fell—and then Amos opened the door. I embarrassed myself in so many ways, Jackie. Instead of acting like a mature woman I reverted back to my high school days."

"Keeva, I think it's great that you actually showed some emotion! You have been a cold, heartless, serial dating bitch since your divorce. I have no idea why Amos has hung in there with you as long as he has. You've treated him like a jump off for months. Our parents did not raise us to act the way you have been acting!"

"Speak for yourself. You and Rena are the only people I know who grew up like the Cosby kids. My mom may have taught me how to act, but my dad didn't teach me shit! The only men who gave me a clue about how a woman should be treated were Uncle Shorty, Uncle Sugar Babe, and Micah. Adaris has started out strong, but you may want to warn him that I am watching his ass like a hawk! They always start out strong but then teeter out in the end."

"That's another thing, Keev, you always expect the worst in people. Like you expected Amos to go home with Jazzmine last night. Anyone can see how much he cares for you. You just need to realize that and decide where to go from there."

"I knew I should have called Max. She would have told me to go slower on this one."

"She probably would have, Keeva, and I don't disagree with that. You don't want to go into another marriage with even more baggage."

"Whoa, girl, slow your roll. I am not talking about marriage here."

"Then what are you talking about? If you didn't care about Amos you wouldn't have showed your ass last night, and you wouldn't be calling me the morning after my wedding reception. You would have called one of those scrubs you used to deal with and spent the day forgetting how stupid you acted last night. Just think about it."

With that Jackie hangs up, turns around in Adaris' lap, and says, "Does Keeva's story sound about like the one you just heard from Amos?"

Adaris leans over and kisses Jackie soundly on the lips, then he says, "Close, but Amos is out for keeps. I still ain't sure yet what the hell Keeva is doing. Aren't you glad we aren't having those problems anymore?"

"Yeah babe. I can't wait to watch as Keeva finds out that the best laid plans of mice and men often go astray."

***

*30 minutes earlier . . .*

"Hey dude, its Amos, what's up!"

"Well, what's up is you are calling and interrupting my time with my wife!"

"I figured the two of you had done all of the boning you needed over the last few weeks. She isn't tired of your old decrepit butt yet dude?"

"Nah, man. I figure my baby won't be tired of me for another 40 or 50 years. What do you want, Hunt?"

"I need to holla at you for a minute about a problem Amos is having."

"Amos, stop talking in third person. I bet your little problem is probably only little in stature and has a personality bigger than the entire state of Tennessee. What did she do now, Hunt?"

"After she ignored me for dang near two weeks, she comes over at about 2:00 this morning and bangs on my door."

"And why would she be banging on your door at that ungodly hour?"

"Maybe because she saw me dancing with Jazz earlier and assumed we were together."

"Well, were you?"

"Not really, man. We were just hanging out and dancing, we didn't leave together."

"Were you supposed to be with Keeva last night?"

"I wasn't even sure if she would acknowledge my presence until I hemmed her up while we were taking pictures."

"Man, will you get to the point?"

"She was jealous, dude. For the first time since I met Keeva eight months ago she actually acted like she gave a damn about me."

"So that's progress, right?"

"Nope."

"Hunt, any other day I would be tremendously patient, but my beautiful wife just finished cooking so get on with it please."

Amos sighs and says, "Over these eight months our relationship has been mostly physical. Sometimes I feel like Keeva has been using me as her jump off."

"So do you want to be more than her jump off?"

"Man, I want to be her moon and her stars. Her beginning and her end, her—"

"I get it man. You want more than just a physical relationship."

"Yeah man, I do. At first it was cool just hanging out, but I realize that Keeva is different than most women. I started teasing her about being my baby's mama but now I really mean that crap."

"Hunt, it's hard to go back. You and Keeva started out like most people do. You got intimate too soon. Once you get involved physically it's more difficult to really get to know each other."

"It wasn't me, man. Keeva made me do it!"

"Whatever, man. I am sure she didn't have to twist your arm. No wonder you feel like a cheap slut. She has got you feenin'. Why don't you go back to the beginning?"

"What do you mean, the beginning?"

"You'll figure it out on your way home."

"What do you mean?"

"Aren't you driving home today?"

"Yeah . . ."

"You'll be on the road for over five hours, which should give you plenty of time to figure it out. One thing I will tell you is this: God did not make man to be a woman. Think about it my friend. I gotta run, my baby is waiting."

I hang up and stare at the phone. What the heck is Dair talking about? First he says go back to the beginning and then he says I'm not meant to be a woman. I have five hours to figure out how not to be Ms. Doubtfire, Madear, Tootsie, and Big Mamma cause I aint going down like the chump that Keeva thinks I am!

# What Number Are You?

After my jacked up conversation with Jackie I got back in bed. Which is what I should have done hours ago. I stayed in bed all day Sunday, and liked it so much I thought I'd shoot for Monday as well. Monday got to feeling so good that I stretched it into an entire week. All that time in bed taught me several things. One, there is nothing but foolishness on TV. As a marketing maven, I really need to do something about improving the commercials. Two, I sure am glad that Jackie is such a great cook. Over the last year she packed my freezer full of yummy food. All I have to do is stick it in the oven or microwave. Three, my mattress sucks.

The "Sleep Number" bed infomercial was one of the few that impressed me, so I decided to order one. I had the nerve to ask them to rush it, so by Monday I was switching from one side to the next to see which number I preferred. During the day, 35 is my favorite. At night, 60 is my number. Since I'm here by myself I figured, why not try both sides? Speaking of by myself, I haven't heard a word from Amos since he went back to Georgia. I am so tempted to reach out to him, but what would I say? "Hey Amos, so glad you made it home. Now when are you coming back to mama to get your purse?"

As the weekend approaches, I decide to shoot for a world record of time spent in bed and return to civilization on Monday.

Just as I'm settling in on the left side of my new purchase, the doorbell rings. Not a lazy single ring but one that won't stop because the idiot on the other side won't take their damn finger off the buzzer! I think, maybe it's Amos, and my heart starts to pound. Maybe he has missed my pocketbook so much that he cut his trip short to come back to me. I run to the door and tear it open. A few things happen. First I see two people who have been the bane of my existence my entire life. Second, my security alarm goes off. Believe me, both scare the shit out of me.

I either have to slam the door in their faces or turn off the alarm. Since I don't want the police to pay me a visit, I choose the alarm. I already avoided a DUI, and I'm not taking any chances. My brother Bo and my cousin Leo barge in. While I love them both with the love of Jesus, I often despise them the way you despise getting a piece of popcorn stuck in your tooth or a corn on your toe. You know the problem is just temporary but will make you feel extremely uncomfortable for a while. Bo is my older brother by three years. You know how people are shocked when they find out who you are related to? Well, I get that reaction all the time. Bo talks constantly, has no filter, and is one of those people who make you want to run when you see them coming because you know you're about to get hemmed up for a long time. Leo . . . well, Leo is Rena and Jackie's brother, sort of. Which would kind of make him my cousin. You know how a family has a secret that is not really a secret but that you don't find out about until it's too late to really change your mental paradigm. Well, that's Leo. He is really Uncle Shorty's sister Lucy's son. Shorty and Aunt Ella adopted him when he was an infant, so he grew up as my cousin. Technically he is really only kin to Rena and Jackie, but since none of us really knew that until we were older, I get to claim him by default as my cousin.

Ironically, Bo and Leo hit it off at a very young age and were inseparable—that is, until Leo got into trouble about four years ago and ended up serving time in federal prison. Uncle Shorty always warned him that if he didn't straighten up he would serve two the hard way. I never knew what that meant until Leo was locked up and Uncle Shorty said, "I told that boy he would serve two the hard way, but he actually served four. It's so much easier to do the right thing so you never have to serve any time at all." Anywho, "four the hard way" and "mouth almighty" have just ambled into my living room, and by the look of it they aren't leaving anytime soon.

"Why are you two ringing my doorbell like you don't have any sense? What the hell do you want?" You see, I have to talk to the two of them like this. Uncle Shorty referred to it as getting some cussing in. It's the only way to communicate with these two.

"Hold up, cuz. We are the only people who get to ask the questions up in this piece. Why haven't you been answering your phone? Kyle says you haven't been at work all week. What's going on?"

"Yeah, sis, you look like hell today and your hair is all jacked up. And why do you have your pajamas on? I got about 30 minutes to report back to Serena, and we ain't leaving until we get some answers."

I stand there looking back and forth between the two of them, and it becomes clear to me that my staycation has just come to a screeching halt. How could I have forgotten to call Serena? I should have known my nosey ass family would send Frick and Frack over here. And now that Leo is majoring in criminal justice, which is hilarious 'cause he's the family's ex-con and he thinks he is Johnny Cochran and has the right to interrogate me. Yes, the ex-con is going to school to help future lawbreakers. He has some spiel about most people in jail shouldn't be there and blah, blah, blah.

Before I can say a word, Bo pipes in again. "You know Serena's ass has us on a timer, so get to talking, sis."

"Well I—"

"You look like death warmed over, girl. You got anything to eat up in this piece?" says Leo.

"Well, if you would give me a chance to—"

The two of them then commence to have a conversation as if I am not in the room. Something about the girl looks bad. And when is the last time she combed her hair? And why hasn't she been returning anyone's phone calls? So, I climb onto my new Sleep Number bed and lie back on the left side—my 35 side—so I can wait for them to finish their conversation, rummage through my refrigerator, and finally realize I have left the room. And then the real barrage begins.

"Sis, I haven't seen you since Jackie's wedding. Where have you been?"

"Bo, we both know the only reason you and Leo really came over here is 'cause Rena has punked you out. You can let her know that I am fine and will be back in the office on Monday. I just needed to get myself together for a few days."

"You were right, cuz," says Leo.

"He was right about what?" I say, swinging around to look at Bo.

"I told the fam you were hiding out over some dude, and after looking at your jacked up hair, the dishes in the sink, and your new mattress, I know I'm right. 'Cause you always keep your hair tight, you never eat at home except what Aunt Ella or Jackie has cooked for you, and you just made an extravagant purchase."

"You think you know me, don't you Bo? Well, you missed a few things during your inspection. I also ordered a number of other items from my two new favorite channels and I'm contemplating getting all my hair cut off."

"Well, since we have about 15 more minutes before Rena calls, why don't you tell me who this chump is so we can decide if we need to kick his ass. I figure if you haven't done any of your jujitsu moves on him yet he is either too quick, too strong, or . . . wait a minute. You must have put your running shoes on again," says Leo.

"Yeah dog, she has done something stupid again and now she's in hiding."

"Keeva, when are you going to learn that running from an uncomfortable situation isn't going to solve anything? Don't you think it's time to face your fear of love and commitment and let Amos take care of you?" Leo asks, shaking his head, clearly disappointed in me.

"Yeah sis, your destructive behavior will only lead you to make irrational decisions. And as a man, I can tell you that we aren't attracted to a woman who has low self-esteem, is wishy washy, or has issues with her age," Bo says. "Just because you are a Gemini doesn't mean you have to be so indecisive."

"You only meet a few single, well-paid, childless, good-looking, college-educated men in your lifetime. You had Damon, and look how that turned out. The odds are against

78

you, so I strongly suggest you get your shit together before Amos moves on with that thick, fine as hell sister he was dancing with last week at the reception," says Leo.

"Now, if that big ass country boy hasn't put his hands on you inappropriately, broken your heart without cause, and ain't harassing you, then we are out of here. So you better speak now or hold your peace, 'cause you know Leo and I are trying not to catch another case, though you know we will for you," says Bo, walking toward my front door.

"She ain't saying nothing, man, so it seems once again we called it. Get yourself together, cuz. You know our family doesn't go down like two flat tires. The big old boy will be back by next week, so go have your wig tightened, paint your face, and get a wax job in all the right places. Let's be out, Bo" says Leo. His phone rings as he walks toward the door.

"Yeah Rena, she is fine. Bo and I just dropped a little knowledge on baby girl and she should be ready by the time Amos gets back in town," Leo says as he follows Bo out to the car.

Just when I think my brother and cousin are hopeless losers, they walk into my house, case the place, eat my food, talk about my hair and my compulsive shopping, and tell me to get my act together before I lose something I never had. Maybe I need to fire my shrink and hire the two of them.

After Bo and Leo leave, I sit around fuming over my nosey, overbearing family. Then I realize that I could have the kind of family that doesn't give a rat's ass if I'm dead or alive in my house or if I am some hoarder burying herself alive. I just read about that woman who was dead in her apartment for over a year before someone noticed, so I'm glad they checked on me.

Instead of calling Rena and cussing her out for sending over the two people who drive me nuts, I do the opposite just to piss her off. I do nothing. Nothing that is, except clean up my kitchen, which I've neglected the last week. Then I put my new 500 count sheets on my Sleep Number mattress. I even decide to take a bath and wash my hair. In the bathroom I take some time to really look at myself. I'm still holding up at age 32 without the assistance of Botox, microdermabrasion, or other augmentation. Thank God for good genes and good bras! But I need to do something different.

My two full walk-in closets—to say nothing of my credit card bill—remind me I don't need to do any shopping. My face is wrinkle-free, thanks to drinking about a gallon of water every day, but my hair . . . I've been growing it out for the last five years and I'm suddenly tired of it. I decide to call my stylist Tia and make an appointment to cut if off. And I know just the place to debut my new do. Aunt Ella is having a cookout at the Plantation—that's what we call her house—next weekend. I have a few days to decide if I wanted to look like Halle,

Rihanna (pre Chris Brown mishap), or the chick named Bird in Soul Food. There is going to be a new woman in town, and Amos Hunter won't know what to do with her!

***

During my last day home in Macon I receive a text from Adaris inviting me to a small gathering Ms. Ella is having at her house before Jackie's sister Serena returns to Chicago. I love the Donovan women. Not only are they gorgeous, kind, and loving but they can also throw down in the kitchen . . . all except Keeva. The cooking gene skipped right over her.

I really miss Keeva. Before I started putting pressure on her to spend time with me we talked all the time. Now that I think back, before I pushed her about settling down and having kids, Keeva and I did a lot of things together. Most other woman would have loved to talk about a future together, but not my Keeva.

It took me the long drive home to figure out what Adaris was trying to tell me. It finally hit me that the only way to win Keeva is to start all over, and that I need to reverse our roles and get us back to the natural order of things. While I was home I took some time to read over the book of Genesis. Adam, while very obedient to God, was the head of his household. Sure, he made some bad decisions, but he took responsibility for them. Eve also had a well-defined role as Adam's helper— to help him create a family. Of course I know times have changed over the last few thousand years, but I also realize that although Keeva is a Renaissance woman she probably also craves loyalty, consistency, and devotion.

While driving it hit me that I need to man up. I've been acting like one big ole punk. I've allowed Keeva to control our relationship and take on the role of the man. Not that I've had any problem being accommodating, but I need to stop letting Keeva think she can run over me and not respect my feelings.

I also realize that Keeva is more attracted to me when my behavior is more dominant and self-confident. I'm learning that caring about someone doesn't mean letting them walk all over you. You also have to express how you feel and set boundaries. Over the years I've let my size put me in a box. I learned to use my size and power on the football field, but off the turf I've turned myself into a bit of a buffoon, thinking that would make people feel more comfortable.

Well, enough of that! It's time I acknowledge that I am 6 feet 7 inches of fabulousness, and   if Keeva can't see it then the hell with her. In the long run I'd be miserable constantly acquiescing to whatever she wants, and by the time she was finished with me I wouldn't have a bit of self-respect left. I am going to turn the tables on Ms. Keeva Hudson-McGhee, and when I finally slow her itty-bitty self down, she is going to drop that hyphenated name and be Keeva Hunter. I am going to work her until she starts eating out of my hand. I will make her see that I am thick and fine and sexy. I will convince her that big is in!

I have 24 hours to get my game plan together. This will be going to a war of the worst kind for Keeva. It is time for a turf war!

# Surprise, Surprise, Surprise

I know this "little gathering" my Aunt Ella is planning will turn into a huge party—my Aunt Ella never does anything small. What with an event planner, a coach and an ex-convict as children you could have a smashing event with a lot of athletes and criminals all in one place. Several years ago, Aunt Ella and Uncle Shorty bought two acres of land in a small subdivision and built what we call "the Plantation," a house that would rival the mansions of the Old South. No one could figure out why they would want to build something reminiscent of the not so good old days, so I decided to ask her what the heck they were thinking. She looked at me calmly and said, "Our forefathers built those houses board by board and brick by brick. They designed them, built them, and then kept them clean—the slave owners didn't lift a finger. Why wouldn't I want to build a home for my family that is in keeping with that tradition? You young people need to get over all of the misconceptions like Uncle Tom, plantation homes and other urban fiction. Reading is fundamental. Before you start talking about my crib, make sure you know the facts."

After that history lesson, I shut my mouth and never said another word; in fact, the Plantation suddenly seemed more beautiful to me than ever, with its big ass porch, lush ferns, and window shutters. And of course Uncle Shorty found a way to "ghettofi" it just enough so we all felt right at home. He threw up a basketball court in the back yard, along with a huge charcoal grill and a sound system that rivals a concert hall.

I know being summoned to Aunt Ella's won't just be about great food and wonderful company. I suspect I'm being set up, like Kunta Kinte was back in the day. Why? Because I haven't heard a word from Jackie or Serena. Not that they would call me about cooking anything—I'm the girl who supplies the paper goods and drinks. It isn't that I can't cook. I actually know how to do a little something in the kitchen, but why try to compete with the master cooks in our family? I figure I can overachieve in another area and save my cooking skills for special times. Rena and Jackie are convinced that the way to a man's heart is through his stomach. You should have seen Jackie caking and baking for Adaris. Come to think of it, she may have been on to something, 'cause I remember a few pairs of shoes, lots of flowers, and, strangely, a whole lot of chewing gum being delivered during their courtship.

On my drive over to Aunt Ella's, I figure I'll call Max to see what she has been up to. She had flown up to New York to spend a few weeks with Chris since she was out of school for the summer and he had a break before the season started.

"Hallo."

"Hey girl. Why do I always feel like when I talk to you, you are singing to me? I just love that little Crucian accent you got going on."

"You know, I almost didn't answer my phone when I saw your ugly face pop up. But since you have a little mud on me, I figured I should make myself available."

"Its a little dirt, Max, and it's good to hear your voice as well. How are you feeling?"

"I am feeling just fine. Why do you ask?"

"You know exactly why I ask! The last time I saw you, we thought you may have a bun in the oven. You know, knocked up!"

"You certainly know how to be a killjoy, don't you Keeva. I am not going to talk about that right now. I only have a few more days left with Chris and I'm trying to keep them as stress free as possible."

"He's close by, isn't he?"

"Yes, stupid! And I hope you plan to be on good behavior today at Ms. Ella's. I hear she's having a cookout and that everyone who is anyone is going to be there. Well, except Chris and me."

"Yeah, if you count a few ex-cons, some fifth cousins, and a few washed up football players, then you got it. It should be loads of fun. The only reason I'm going is for the food. I can see the rest of those people anytime."

"Um hmm . . . well, since you haven't seen Amos in a while, you need to get yourself together and make sure you have your face in the place at a respectable time."

"Have you been talking to Amos, Max?"

"My baby has talked to him a few times, and that's all I am saying, girl," Max says with a chuckle.

"This conversation is far from over, and we need to talk before your body starts to do the talking for you, if you get my drift. I would say "don't do anything I wouldn't do," but it's too late for that! Oh, and don't play me close. I certainly plan to make an entrance today."

"I'll talk to you when I get back to the mainland. Love you girl—tell everyone we said hello." Max sounds tired all of a sudden.

"No matter what, it's going to work out, Max. I love you too, girl," I say while wondering if that will apply to me as well.

I pull up to the Plantation and take a deep breath. Every time I come to my Aunt's house I get nostalgic. There are a lot of memories in this place; many of them centered on the king of our family, my Uncle Shorty. I wonder what he would say about my situation. Probably something like, "Keeva, don't be afraid to roll the dice. You can't win if you never play. Scared money don't win, baby." Now that I think about it, most of his words of advice were centered on some type of sport or game. The athletic gene did not rub off on me, but the competitive gene sure as hell did. So why am I sitting here acting like a punk? This is my house! Well, it's actually my aunt's house, but if anyone should be scared about going in, it should be Amos and not me! I am going to roll the dice, but I pray I don't crap out and roll a seven. And if Amos has the nerve to bring anyone with him, I may just become a boxer! Wait a minute—how do I know he's even coming today? I haven't heard a word from Jackie since the day after her reception, and the only word I had from Amos was the text he sent when he got home.

Well, there's nothing to it but to do it. I can't sit in my pearl white Jaguar XJ all day. I have to find out if my broken up boo is in the house. I'm wearing a blue jean dress that stops at my knees, along with a pair of 4-inch black sandals to add a little height. I reach back to flip my hair out of the way and there's nothing there—I suddenly remember that my hair is now cropped very short. Why in the hell did I pick today of all days to debut a new look? I must be out of my mind. Someone must have slipped me a hair mickey to make me do something that stupid!

When the girls in the salon told me how beautiful I looked and how my new haircut accentuates my pretty gray eyes, I sucked it in. I told myself, "You do look good, from head to toe. From the top of your newly shorn head to the bottom of your freshly pedicured feet." But as I start moving toward the house, I hear my Gemini "bad twin" say, "What made you cut your hair off after all these years? Are you sick? Now you look like a boy." But no, I wasn't sick, just temporarily insane.

***

Why I allowed Adaris and Shelley to convince me to come to Ms. Ella's house, I will never know. Actually, I didn't have much of a choice. Shelley is still my team captain and Dair used to be, so how could I say no? Besides, this is not the time or place to have a confrontation with Keeva. I haven't had any contact with her during the two weeks I was gone, and I really needed that time to screw my head back on straight and figure out my game plan. And I'm sure not one to turn down an invite to enjoy the Donovan women's amazing food.

It's been quite a while since I had a chance to sit down with my ole girlfriend, Aunt D, who is Ms. Ella's oldest sister. I have no idea how old either of them is because all the women in that family seem to guard their age with their life, except Jackie of course, since hers is public knowledge since her WNBA days. You also can't tell their ages because all the women in the Donovan family are aging so beautifully. Jackie's mom is a straight fox. If I weren't so crazy about Keeva I would holler at her! Well, in truth I wouldn't holler at Ms. Ella, but she is easy on the eyes.

Aunt D and I met when I went over to Jackie's house one night to pick up a Christmas gift for Adaris. Jackie had convinced me to sneak a photo album into Adaris' carry-on bag before we left for an away game. That was the first time I actually saw Adaris get emotional, and I knew then that he was in love with Jackie. Heck, I shed a few tears myself. Seeing the time and love Jackie put into that album made me realize that, while most football players have a lot of money and notoriety, all most of us really wanted is for someone to give a damn about us.

So, when I rang the doorbell of Ms. Ella's house, this vision that, despite being in her eighties is still a real beauty, opened the door. I swear it was love at first sight, for both of us. She looked at me and said, "Um, um, um, if I was about 20 years younger I would climb you like a tree and sit on one of your branches." Then she reached over and gave me a big hug, and I swear she rubbed her hand on my back, slid it down, and pinched my butt! I was hooked—I figured anyone old enough and bold enough to pinch Amos' behind was worth spending a little time with. I also sensed she was cheering Keeva and me on. I had no idea if she knew how hooked I was on Keeva at the time, but she found ways to offer me up antidotes to both encourage me and warn me.

I am here for some good home cooking, to sneak a peek at Ms. Ella, and spend time with my cougar, Aunt D. In that order. If I happen to run across Keeva, I swear I won't sweep her up in my arms and try to ravish her! At least that is what I am telling myself. Before Keeva decided to start acting like the dude in our relationship, we had become very comfortable with each other. But since I decided to go cold turkey to keep myself from feeling like a two dollar hoe I've really been feeling the need to see her.

I decide to come a little early so I can help Adaris and Shelley do some grilling. I'm not sure how Adaris took over the grill, since everyone knows Jackie is the grill master. I heard that the first meal she ever fed Adaris was one she cooked on the grill, which hooked him like a fish. She had his nose so wide open after he tasted her meat that he was damn near stupid over the last year.

Anyhow, I stay by the grill supervising the chefs until I hear my cougar come outside and greet me.

"Um, um, um, if I could get rid of the ten men who were yanking on my skirt, I would grab you and make you mine."

I turn around and give Aunt D the big bear hug she is waiting on, and suddenly realize why people love to be around her. She knows how to make a man feel good about himself. I secretly wish she would have some extra sessions with Keeva!

"Well you two, as much as Amos would like to stay out here giving you grilling instructions, my Aunt D has come to get me and I must go!"

"Yeah, go back in the house so Ms. Ella can fawn all over you and the fresh vegetables you brought, you kiss as—"

"Hey, watch your mouth, man! We have an elder out here," says Adaris, smiling at Aunt D while giving her a peck on the cheek.

"Watch your mouth, Dair. I'm not much older than the three of you—put together! But as I always say, it's not how old you are, it's how young you feel."

"That's right honey," I say, looping my arm around Aunt D's to walk her back into the house. "I will see you two chumps later. I need to spend some time with my baby before she goes back to Chicago. I think Tiffany and Jackie will be out in a few minutes so Jackie can take over the grill."

"You got jokes, don't you Hunt. Let's see if you are laughing when the fireworks go off in the house in the next hour," Shelley says, chuckling.

"Tell me, my dear, how are you doing? I haven't seen you since we danced at the reception," Aunt D says as we amble back toward the house.

"I'm doing great Aunt D. I went home for a few weeks to visit my family. I worked on the farm, ate off the land, and rested my body."

"Well, my darling, you certainly feel great," Aunt D says, gently squeezing my arm. "But your eyes look a little sad. Is there anything we need to talk about?"

"You know I don't want to talk out of school, Aunt D, but I've been having a few issues with your smallest and most boisterous niece."

"Well, my beloved, sometimes love requires putting your foot down. I love my niece—she reminds me so much of my baby sister—but she has lived a tough life. She has always had the material things and the fierce love of our family, but she has been hurt by men. It started with her father, then her ex-husband. She needs a mature man to handle her, son. You gotta take it slow with that niece of mine, Amos, because if you are playing for keeps you have to play a little chess."

"I was with you until you said chess, Aunt D."

"Chess is a complicated game that has a king and a queen, some pawns, and a few other pieces. You have to be very careful what moves you make, and when, because in the background she is planning her own moves. Get your house in order because that will be an important part of your strategy. Most of all, remember that the key to winning the game is to get a "checkmate," which means that someone has to let go of their pride, vanity, stubbornness and a whole lot of other stuff. My money is on you, honey—now go and get your queen, my king."

By the time Aunt D finishes taking me to school and giving me some homework, we're back inside the house. She gives me one final squeeze and pat and moves into the kitchen to join the rest of the people who have gathered there.

# Stairway to Heaven

I always wonder why people are so darn loud at my aunt's house. It doesn't matter if they're happy, sad, or even mad. I'm not sure if they talk so loudly because the joy at seeing each other or if they're trying to be heard over the roar of the crowd. As I move toward the kitchen I take one last deep breath to tamp down my nerves. I'm not sure what the reaction will be to my short hair, but I do know that when Jackie cut off a chunk of her hair during her first basketball season it nearly caused a riot. But it wasn't the fact that she cut her hair but that she cut it for the very first time—at age 28! So, now me. I feel strangely liberated and so exposed all at the same time. You can really hide some things behind long hair, like a jacked up neck or acne on your forehead, or even a crossed eye—thankfully I have none of those. With a short cut you also feel as if a huge weight has been removed from your shoulders. It's a shame that I didn't think to do this years ago. Both Aunt Ella and Serena have been sporting short haircuts for years and they look fabulous. So, now I have short hair to match my short stature, and all of a sudden I also have a short temper—I walk in the kitchen and the first thing I see is Amos leaning down to give my Aunt D a kiss on her cheek, and her giving him the old rub, pat, and slide.

I'm in such a haze that I don't hear Aunt Ella, Jackie, Tiffany, and Serena all make on about my new haircut. By the time I start to bask in the love I am getting for my new do, I suddenly feel Amos' eyes on me. I turn around and see him staring at me so intensely that it gives me pause. He slowly runs his eyes from the top of my newly shorn head to my just polished feet. He lingers on my legs as if he is starving. I figure that while I have his full attention I will give him something to think about, as payback for him leaving me to my own devices for the last two weeks. I do what any self-respecting hussy would do. I bend over to pick up the cups and plates I dropped on the floor when I walked in so he'd get a good look at my rump shaker, and my calves as well. I add a few moves some dancer friends had given me, and as I'm coming up from a toe touch I hear a whoosh of air from across the room. I got him! I haven't lost my touch after all.

The attention doesn't stay on my new hairdo for long. Amos is the only piece of testosterone in the room, which means all the attention is turned on him. While everyone is fawning over him and thanking him for the homegrown vegetables and fruit he brought from Georgia, I steal a look at him. My goodness he does look good. I'd forgotten how massive he is in person. He towers easily over everyone in the room—hell everyone in the state. But, he wears his giant size with a gracefulness that is so damn sexy, and I get turned on just watching him from across the room. The smirk on his face gives me every indication that he knows it. Damn him! So I say, "Amos, what the hell are you doing standing in the middle of my aunt's kitchen with all of these hens? Is there something you need to tell us?"

"It's good to see you too, Keeva."

"Humph. You could have fooled me," I say, folding my arms across my chest.

Amos smirks again and folds his massive arms across his chest. "Why would you say something like that, little bit?"

"You can cut the words of endearment, Amos. I am not in the mood for that today. It's not so good to see you, even after two weeks," I say, stomping out to the great room.

"The next move is yours, Amos. Go get your queen. But remember what we discussed outside. One false move can get you beat," Aunt D whispers in Amos' ear.

"Since I am the king, Aunt D, how about I give my queen a few minutes to cool down," Amos says with a chuckle.

Aunt D looks up at Amos and says, "Are you using me as a pawn?"

"Of course I am Aunt D. I have eight to use, don't I? And I learned from the best, right?"

About five minutes later, Amos finds me in the basement still stewing.

"Little bit, your blood pressure would be much easier to manage if you didn't stay pissed off at me half the time," Amos says as he walks up to me. "What made you decide to get your nappy dugout cut?"

"Would you stop calling me little bit? And what the hell is a nappy dugout?"

Amos slowly ambles over to me, puts his big hands on the back of my head, and gathers me closer to him. God he smells heavenly—a mix between charcoal, sweat, and Drakkar— damn, that amazing old cologne again! Then he starts massaging my scalp, and as I slowly lean closer to his chest, I suddenly remember my angst.

"Well, beautiful, a nappy dugout is what us country folks call your haircut. I love it by the way, even though you didn't consult me before you cut off all that wonderful hair. Now what am I going to hold onto when we're . . . well, you know."

"Consult with you! How in the hell does a woman consult you when you won't even talk to her?"

Amos takes a deep breath and pulls me closer. "Just say hi, Amos. I missed you. Why did it take you so long to see me? Say it, Keeva. It won't hurt you to admit that you missed me over the last two weeks, 'cause I sure as hell missed you."

Amos starts kissing me, first at the top of my head and then on my forehead. I finally say, "Ok, you big oaf, hi, it's good to see you."

98

"What about the 'I missed you' part, Keeva?" Amos says, again massaging the back of my head and pulling me closer.

"Shut up, Amos, and just kiss me. Damn!"

As he inches closer to my lips he says, "You are way too pretty to be talking so ugly. Don't worry, Amos will give you what you need."

After that we don't make any noise for a while, unless you count some moaning. Oh Lord, that is actually me moaning. For one so young, Amos sure knows how to play me like a drum. Just as I'm about to wrap my arms around his waist to get a little closer, he steps back.

"Keeva that was just a hello kiss. You won't get anything else from Amos. I'm saving myself for my girlfriend."

"Your girlfriend. I thought I was . . ."

"You thought what, Keeva? Are you ready to take the next step and be my girl, or are you just using me for a few moments of pleasure?"

"You didn't seem to have any problem shaking the sheets with me a few weeks ago, Amos. What has changed your mind? Did you rekindle a relationship with one of those country ass girls you used to date?" I say, throwing my hip out and putting my hands on them both like an angry black woman.

"It's really none of your business what I did in the last few weeks, little bit. Just know that my priorities have shifted and I

99

am now playing for keeps. Let me give you something to think about while you decide if you want to stop trying to be the man in our relationship and relinquish those rights to me," Amos says. He grabs my arms and picks me up off the floor so I am at eye level with him. "But just know this, Keeva Hudson-McGhee, I am not going to play any more head games with you. I am serious about what I want in my life, and if you can't give it to me, then you are not the woman God ordained me to be with." With that he backs me up against the wall and kisses me speechless. Before I know, it my dress is above my hips and my legs are wrapped around Amos' waist. The three buttons at the top of my dress are unbuttoned, my bra is scrunched over to the left, and by the time he puts me back on the floor I am speechless and damn near naked. I was well into my second climb up the stairway to heaven!

As Amos walks back up the steps to the kitchen, I hear him say, "Think about it, babe. Amos is a great catch. I would hate for you to miss out on me because you have too much pride to admit that you actually care about someone other than yourself."

Thirty minutes later, once my pulse has finally slowed down and my pocketbook has stopped quivering, I comb what little hair I have left back in place, straighten my clothes, and walk up the stairs toward the kitchen—and right smack into Serena.

"Hmm . . . looks like someone just returned from the den of sin. The look on your face is somewhere between shock, pissed, and horny. Funny thing is, I just saw Amos a few minutes ago and he looked calm, happy, and satisfied. Wonder what that was all about, little cuz!" Serena says, walking away with a bellow of laughter.

"Go to hell, Rena!"

Before I enter the kitchen, who is standing there but Noah, Jackie's 15-year-old sort of step-son.

"What's up, Ma," Noah says, with a smile on his face.

"I am not your mama, literally or figuratively, so I would suggest you stop with the words of endearment," I say with a sigh. "What can I do for you, Noah?"

"What you can do, shorty, is tell me what the hell you were doing downstairs with Amos. What does he have that I don't have?"

Is this child kidding me? Now the old Keeva of a week ago would have cut him to the quick, but the new Keeva . . . well, here goes. Before I can remind him that Amos is of legal age, 200 pounds heavier, has a huge bank account, and a few other things that are huge, it hits me that there is nothing wrong with Amos. But there is obviously something wrong with me. Out of the mouth of this babe has come a question that shows me Amos really could be the one. Just when I'm feeling warm and fuzzy about Noah, the little creep puts his finger to my lips and says, "Shorty, you never answered my question."

I roll my eyes and take a deep breath, then I smile. I realize my words could have a huge impact on his self-esteem and how he treats girls in the future, so I say, "Noah, Amos and I were having a talk." All right, I stretched the truth a little, but he didn't need to hear more. "You're a handsome, smart young man, and I'm honored that you think so much of me, but there a few things that would make a relationship with you a bit of a challenge."

"Tell me what they are, baby, 'cause your boy can fix it," Noah says, moving his finger from my lips to the side of my face.

I remove Noah's hand from my face and squeeze it. "The first thing is our age difference. You are 15 and I am, well, I'm over the age of 18. In the state of Tennessee anything between us is illegal."

"But shorty—"

Deep breath. "My name is Keeva. There are hundreds of young ladies out there who would be happy to be with you. We can be friends and see each other at events like these. After all, we're practically related—your brother's father is married to my first cousin. And doesn't Sophia have a younger sister? Maybe you and A.J. can double date!"

"You mean Sabrina? She's cool but I like older women. Just tell me that you have another man and I am too late," Noah says with a frown.

I squeeze Noah's hand even tighter because at this point I want to break it, but then I remember that this is a character-building moment. "Yes, Noah, I have someone else I am trying to spend time with, and I really want to focus on one person at a time."

"Is it Amos?" Noah asks with a sigh.

"It's complicated Noah, but, yes, I am interested in Amos."

"But what, Keeva?"

"But I am not sure if Amos still feels the same way."

"I knew he was my competition. If he doesn't realize how perfect you are it's his loss. And if he does anything to mistreat you I will kick his big ass." Then he leans down, kisses me on the cheek, and walks away.

Somehow Noah got it both so right and so wrong. Everything he just said about Amos should have been said about me. My actions over the last month may have very well caused me to lose Amos.

After that little chat, I figure it's time for me to break camp and head home to get my bearings. Between Amos, Serena, and now Noah, I have had enough. And then I run into Jackie's ass!

"Hey cuz, where are you stomping off to so fast?"

"I was actually thinking about blowing this Popsicle stand."

"We haven't eaten yet! I just went outside to stop Adaris and Shelley from burning the meat on the grill. They were so busy talking about their new business venture that . . . wait a minute what's wrong? You never miss a meal."

"Let's see, Amos talked nasty to me, groped me up, and then walked out on me. Rena just did what she always does, made fun of me. And Noah just gave me a psych session about the state of my relationship or lack thereof. And you, who are so blindly in love, if you let that dude better known as your husband burn my ribs I am going to beat you down."

"Don't try to divert me by talking about my meat, girl!"

"Stop being nasty for a minute Jackie. Ain't nobody got time for that," I say, balling my hands into fists.

"Well, I was talking about the meat on the grill, not my husband . . . but let's talk about you."

"Let's not talk about me. I know you do a really good job of getting your prayers through, 'cause after that last year you had, God has truly blessed you. So please, just spend a few more seconds on your girl. I have a lot of decisions to make about my future and I really have no idea what to do."

"Well, if you're contemplating a future with Noah, then you better go talk to Leo. He can give you the best advice on how to make it in prison. If you are contemplating one with Amos, then I not only will pray for you, I will also cheer for you. He is

104

a wonderful man. By the way, love your haircut, and so does Amos, obviously. I would suggest you stop by the bathroom and comb what's left of your hair," Jackie says, then she quickly turns to go back outside.

# Game Changers

"Hey Hunt, where you been, man? You know we need you out here to keep us from burning this meat. Did Jackie come and get you?" says Shelley with a big grin.

"You know that big punk had to go in and kiss up to my mother-in-law and all the other women in the house. You are such an overachiever, man. Always bringing organic home-grown shit around. Do you realize my wife is going to try to convince me to plant a garden in our yard? And you know she can get me to do anything," says Adaris.

"That's what happens when you wait until after you are married to do the do. Anyone that can make you wait a year to get it can make you do anything," laughs Amos. "And hey, I figure if all the other woman in the family love me, maybe one day Keeva's little ass will get a clue."

"Hmm . . . well, if it doesn't work out with Keeva there's always Aunt D. She is amazing. I pray that Jackie is that wonderful when she's in her eighties."

"So, what did I miss while I was inside?" says Amos.

"Actually, Shelley and I were out here talking about a business venture we've been considering. Since I decided to forgo that job with ESPN during my first year of marriage, I'm currently jobless. As much as I love being a house husband, I don't want my wife to get used to me keeping a spotless house and tending to the boy," laughs Adaris.

"Tell me about it. I have been looking for a good investment," says Amos.

"Remember when you came into the league a few years ago and went from a few dollars in your pocket to a few million dollars in the bank? Well, if it weren't for people like Shelley and myself who had mercy on your big ass, you'd soon be back where you started a few years ago. You probably would have bought about six cars and a motorcycle or two, and some realtor would have put you up in a high-end rented house."

"And when you had to retire because someone bigger and faster was coming up behind you, you'd be homeless, carless, moneyless, and, by the looks of things, womanless," says Shelley.

"Get to the point, you old bastards," says Amos.

"The two of us and our boy Chris Map are creating a nonprofit to help athletes manage their money so they can live comfortably during their careers and after."

"So, are you aiming to replace all the CPAs, attorneys, sports agents, and investment advisors of the world?" Amos asks.

"Nah man, not that. Those people make the world go around. We want to present examples of people who did it wrong and then show how to do it right. We plan to ask the best and brightest to do seminars and one-on-one sessions. Between the three of us we've gotten about 30 people we consider trustworthy advisors. Think about it man. Most of our peers are always griping about their agent, attorney, CPA, or banker, and those people just have too much control over our shit. The short list of people we've lined up are great at what they do, but they also have a leadership mentality. They do what they do not to gain notoriety but to help people make the best choices. One of those people just so happens to be my mother-in-law, and she didn't do it by studying to be a stock broker. She read books, took courses, and studied the market. How do you think my in-laws got this beautiful home? It wasn't paid for with a teacher's salary."

"Dair, that sounds like a great idea, man. What can I do to help?"

"Well, at this point, nothing. A group named GameChangers found out what the three of us are doing and sent us a donation for $25,000 to help with the startup expenses. According to our business plan, we won't need more than $100,000 to get everything up and running. I'll be the only one actively involved in the business, since Chris and Shelley are still in the league. But they both will serve on the advisory board, and so will you if you want to join in. I also asked Jackie and one of her basketball buddies to serve so we can have woman's perspective. Women tend to struggle with these issues more than men because they don't make as much money. Coach Thomas has already given the nod for me to use the Trailblazers as a pilot."

"Who are these GameChanger people? Didn't they also give Jackie's basketball team a sizeable donation last year?"

"Yeah man. All I know is that they are a nonprofit created to help athletes prosper on and off the playing field. They're chartered here in Tennessee but have helped teams and players all around the world—in the last two years they've donated millions of dollars. They work discretely, with no advertising—it's the damndest thing I've ever seen, man."

"We were actually prepared to pay the startup costs out of our pockets until we could get our 501c3 status, so the donation really helps. Not to mention being able to use the GameChangers name."

"It's an awesome idea, especially since so many athletes are people of color and need the most help," says Amos.

"You got it, Hunt. You know, I couldn't really figure out why I had so much trouble coming to an agreement with ESPN. Now I know it's because I was meant to be doing this venture and really helping people who need it. Once we get this going we'll start working with college and high school athletes too. As long as we continue to offer our services for free we should be able to navigate the college sports regulations."

"So, Shelley man, I guess this means you are retiring soon, right? And my boy World, too? Damn, I am going to miss you guys."

"The idea is for us to be around even after we retire. We plan to be the watchdogs of football and then spread out to other sports as well, so don't be getting all mushy and shit on us Hunt."

"Well, count me in for both the advisory board and as a client. I want to know all the ins and outs of my future business venture. But you're gonna need to add gardening and cooking classes to the curriculum and make sure both of you sit at the front of the class—you can't cook worth a damn! Move over Shelley, I got the grill. Now take your butts into the house and check on your wives!"

***

After talking with Jackie I'm debating if I should leave, and then the doorbell rings. Ok, Lord, I get the hint, I guess you're telling me to answer the door. I yell out "I got it!" I open the door and find myself face to face with a very distinguished man. He looks to be in his sixties, with a graying fade haircut. He is impeccably dressed in golf attire and is wearing some magnificent eyeglasses. As I stand there wondering why he looks familiar, he sticks out his hand and says, "You must be Keeva. I have been looking forward to meeting you."

Now, I never really met my father. I heard he was a good-looking man but that things didn't work out between him and my mother. I do know that he's still alive, but I just haven't had the heart or the desire to try to get back all the lost years. I was going to kill my family if they had punked me and set me up to meet him today! I look at him warily and say, "And how do you know who I am, sir?"

"Well, Ella talks about her girls all the time, and she described you exactly right—except it looks like you lowered your ears since the reception."

First it's "nappy dugout" and now "lowered my ears." What is it with these country ass men? And did he say since the reception? Did I see him at the reception?

"Young lady, my name is Johnny Fulton, and I am a friend of your Aunt Ella's. She invited me over today to join you for dinner."

Wait a damn minute! Did he just say Johnny Fulton? As my mind starts going back, I remember meeting a Johnnie Fulton—Johnnie with an *ie*—at the football game several many months ago. I also recall Jackie telling me that a lady Johnnie with an *ie* worked for the architectural firm that designed the house Adaris built. But what the hell is this older male Johnny doing standing on my Aunt Ella's porch looking all fine?

"Well, nice to meet you Mr. Fulton. Did you say you were here to see Aunt Ella?" I take his hand and gently guide him into the house."

"Yes I am, but I'm also looking forward to seeing Adaris and Jackie and the rest of the family. I didn't get a chance to visit with them during the reception."

It suddenly hits me that I did see Aunt Ella talking to a very handsome man at the reception. And said man also caught the garter. I swing around and face Mr. Fulton and hit him with a barrage of questions.

"Mr. Fulton, I do remember seeing you at the reception. Are you Johnnie's father?"

"Yes I am. I also have two other daughters."

"Now, how long did you say you have known Aunt Ella?"

"Well, I actually didn't say, but I met your Uncle Shorty first. You see, Shorty, my wife, and I grew up together on Murphy Street."

"Your wife? Well, where is she?" I ask, looking around as if she will suddenly appear.

"My Margaret passed away about five years ago," he says with a gentle smile.

Now I have really put my foot in my mouth. I realize I'm still holding on to Mr. Fulton's hand, which is oddly very calming. What is with me today?

"So how did you say you met my aunt?"

"Well, I've always been close to both your aunt and uncle. In fact, I helped them design this house many years ago. When my wife passed away, Shorty really helped me heal. After he died I invited Ella to join my grief support group, and she started attending the meetings."

"How interesting. So what are your intentions with my aunt, Mr. Fulton?"

"Well young lady, your aunt is a beautiful, intelligent woman, among other things. Ella and I are friends. My intention at this point is to continue to spend time with her and get to know her family. Where we go from there is largely up to your aunt. It's only been a year and a half since Shorty passed away, and Ella is still healing. In fact, I am not sure you ever really get over such a loss."

"So basically, Mr. Fulton, you're saying it's none of my business," I say with a smile.

Mr. Fulton grabs my other hand, leans over, and kisses me on the cheek. "You remind me so much of my baby girl Johnnie. Beautiful, smart, and always on ten. To be honest with you Keeva, I'm not sure where our friendship will lead, but I do know that I smell something heavenly coming from the kitchen."

Mr. Fulton releases my hands, looks up, and gives someone behind me one of the sweetest smiles I've seen in a long time. And then I hear, "Skip, welcome to our home. I see you have met my niece Keeva. Come and let me fix you a plate and introduce you to the rest of the family and my friends."

As they walk away I suddenly realize that, with or without me, life is moving on. Aunt Ella is forging a new and different relationship with someone other than my uncle. Jackie has moved on with the man she adores. Max and Chris are doing well, but I am stuck. Even my Aunt D recognizes the power of influence and attraction—and she didn't get that from any new age book. The difference between me and them is they embrace it, while I have been fighting it tooth and nail. And what do I have to show for that? A Sleep Number mattress covered with expensive sheets, but the bed is empty. As I turn around and head back toward the kitchen, I realize that I really need to talk to the family matriarchs—they obviously have it going on. It's time for a hen party of monumental proportions.

# A Gathering of Old Hens

By the time I meander back to the kitchen, all the testosterone has blessedly gone back outside to watch Adaris and Shelley burn the meat. The first person I see when I walk in is Aunt D. Somehow she can get away with doing absolutely nothing but dispense advice.

"Keeva, your hair looks like that Halle Berry girl, except you are much prettier. If I had legs like yours they would be wrapped around some handsome young man," Aunt D says, giving me a big smile.

"Speaking of which, Aunt D, I saw you over there a while ago talking and rubbing on Amos. What were you two talking about?"

"We were talking about the game of life, young lady. That Amos is such a young man but wise beyond his years."

"He's wise all right, Aunt D. Over the last few weeks he's been wisely avoiding me like the plague."

"That's funny. I would swear he just told me that he went home to Georgia to spend time with his family for a few weeks. How is that avoiding you, Keeva?" Aunt Ella asks.

"Well Aunt D, I didn't hear one word from him the entire time he was in Georgia. And if I hadn't run into him today, I'm not sure if we would have talked at all."

Rena pipes in with a confused look. "Didn't you tell us at Jackie's reception that you were going to break up with Amos?"

Jackie says, "Well ladies, my favorite cousin had decided she was going to turn Amos loose the night of our wedding reception but it looks like he flipped the script on her."

"I'm afraid to ask you what happened, Keeva, but I sense that we are about to hear all the details," Aunt Ella says, stirring her famous potato salad.

"Yes, you should be, 'cause something obviously jumped off downstairs in Shorty's Shack a little bit ago—Amos came out looking like a peacock and Keeva's hair was jacked up," says Rena.

"And then Noah, Keeva's 15-year-old wonder kid, also broke up with her, so it looks like all of her men have abandoned her," says Jackie.

"Well now, it looks like you girls have it all figured out. Everyone except Keeva. Is that about right baby?" asks Aunt Ella.

"Yeah, that's about right. I was hoping you could drop a little knowledge on me Aunt D. By the way, I met Mr. Fulton a few minutes ago . . ."

"Johnny Fulton is out of your league, darling. I think you first need to figure out if you want to be Amos' acquaintance or his friend."

"What's the difference, sister?" Ella says with a big grin.

"Thanks for asking, little sister. You see, an acquaintance is someone you can take or leave. You spend time with them because they have something that makes you want to keep them close at hand . . . at least for a little while. They can easily be replaced by the next intriguing face.

"But a friend, now that's a different thing. A friend is someone you look forward to seeing and feel a little sad when they leave. A friend is someone you trust with your head and your heart; someone you can be vulnerable around. You might even let them see you at your weakest moment. The Bible even says a friend sticks closer than a brother. What you need to figure out, my darling, is if you want Amos to be your friend or an acquaintance."

"So what are you trying to tell me, Aunt D?"

"What I am saying, honey, is that Amos is not the acquaintance type. He's steady, permanent, reliable, and trustworthy."

"That sounds boring to me, Aunt D."

"Oh, it's far from boring. You see acquaintances are unpredictable, untrustworthy, and fickle. You just need to decide what you want Keeva. I have a feeling the things that make you and Amos so different are the very things that attract you to each other the most."

"So now that Amos has me at arm's length, what do I do Aunt D?"

"Let me take this one, sis. What you do is play some defense, little one, because defense always wins the game. Amos is going to expect you to be loud, obnoxious, and vindictive, so do the unexpected. You see?"

"Damn, Aunt Ella, is that what you think about me? Wait a minute, is that what all of you think about me? That I'm loud and obnoxious and . . .?" I look warily around the room at my family.

"What we think, Keeva, is that life has hardened you a little bit against most people outside your family. Well, I take that back; you're a little rough on Bo and Leo, too. But I digress. You can't put everyone in the same box. Amos is a great guy, and he clearly wants to settle down soon. You are his pick, Keeva. But let me warn you, men will settle for number two or even five if the one woman they want is unobtainable. Men like Amos aren't meant to be alone," says Aunt D.

"And I would add that you need to stop running, Keeva," says Jackie.

"So you want me to change?" asks Keeva with a frown.

"If changing means you stop acting like you have a penis, then most definitely. How you act in the boardroom is not synonymous with how you should act in the bedroom," says Serena.

"So I should join the choir like you, Rena? Cook for my man every day like you, Jackie? Look immaculate like you, Aunt Ella, all while rubbing, patting, and smiling, Aunt D?"

"Be careful, young lady. Them's fighting words," Aunt Ella says with a raised brow.

"I've got this, boo," says Aunt D with a chuckle. "We all know you can't sing worth a damn, Keeva. We also know that you can cook, maybe not as good as those two over there, but you can hold your own. You can go ahead and throw thinly veiled insults at us—or as you young people would say, "Throw some shade"—but you need to take a page from our book, young playa. You modern ladies act like it's a big deal to have a husband, work, have children, and keep a home. Well, that ain't nothing. It's been done since the beginning of time. And we've managed to look good while doing it. Read Proverbs 31 when you get a minute. Now that sister was really holding it down!"

"Keeva honey, no one is asking you to change. We want you to be yourself. Go back to the way you were before Damon tainted you. Let your guard down and be the caring loving, giving woman you have always been. There is nothing wrong with that, no matter what all these liberated women tell you. Stick with your protective behavior and you'll look up one day and find yourself liberated, lonely, and loveless. Oh, and by the way, the rub, pat, and slide had your man eating out of my sister's hand an hour ago," says Aunt Ella.

While we've been talking we have finished up the sides to go with the meat, so we all head outside. We enjoy a wonderful meal and then watch the boys and men play some basketball. I decide to sneak out before the end of the game. I just don't want any more confrontations with Amos, Noah, or even Mr. Fulton.

When I open the car door, I find a bounty sitting on the passenger seat. It's a Longaberger basket filled with strawberries, tomatoes, corn, cucumbers, blackberries, blueberries, and other fresh items in a gorgeous bundle that looks like an expensive flower arrangement.

Tucked between the strawberries is a note that says, "Keeva, I picked all of these vegetables from my private garden. They are as beautiful and fragrant as you are. I hope you enjoy eating them as much as I enjoyed picking them. Amos."

I pick up a strawberry and take a bite of the sweet, juicy fruit . . . and then I cry for the first time in a long time. I pray that I can figure out how to be a virtuous woman like the woman in Proverbs, and I give thanks for the simple but oh so complicated man that God had put in my life. And as I wonder what the hell I am going to cook for my 6-foot-7 farmer from Macon, my tears turn to laughter.

Ella and Aunt D gather at the window to watch Keeva as she walks to her car. Ella turns to Dorthea and says, "Do you think the fruit is going to get her?"

"Yeah, baby sis. Amos is now the one with all the power. I just pray that he uses his power for good," Aunt D says. She gives Ella a hug and they walk back to the kitchen.

# Jilted

I wait about 12 hours before I call Jackie. I need some ideas about what to do with the bounty that Amos left in my car.

"Hello."

"Hey cuz, what's cooking?"

"Hey girl, I actually just got back from the gym. What's cooking with you?"

"That's the problem. Nothing, but I need your help. Yesterday Amos left a basketful of fruit and vegetables in my car."

"Oh Keeva, that is really sweet. One thing about Amos is, you will never go hungry, girl."

"Yes I will, if you don't help me cook it. I want to call Amos and invite him to dinner tonight, so I need you to come over and whip up something for me."

"Ok, I'll come over, but you will be doing the cooking. You know the best way to keep a man is to cook for him."

"That's what you think. I have some ideas that are a lot better."

"You may get him that way, but you have to be more than a one trick pony to keep him. Call Amos, make the date, and if he accepts I'll head over in a few hours."

"Why do I need to call? Can't I send a text?"

"You obviously didn't listen to a word Mom and Aunt D said yesterday, cuz. Change your routine a little. The last thing he will expect is a phone call or a home-cooked meal . . . at least not from you."

"I see, you got jokes! Ok, I'll call him, and he will come because once I tell him I plan to cook he won't be able to stay away."

"Let's hope your confidence extends to your cooking, or he may be in trouble," Jackie says, then hangs up the phone.

***

"Hello."

"Hello Amos, this is Keeva."

"I know who this is. What's up baby girl?"

"I want to thank you for the fruit and vegetables, and the beautiful basket. I also called to see if you want to come over for dinner this evening?"

"You want me to stop by and pick something up, as usual?"

"Well, actually I thought I'd cook for you. Show you I have some skills in the kitchen."

"Now that's funny—this I have got to see. What time?"

"How about you come around seven?"

"Umm . . . let me move some things around and I will be there. Should I bring anything?"

"No, just bring yourself and your appetite."

Jackie stops by around four o'clock and helps me prepare a beautiful salad with the vegetables, topped with a strawberry vinaigrette dressing. We make mashed potatoes, fried corn, and she shows me how to cut up and fry a chicken. For dessert we use the blackberries to make a simple cobbler. We use up everything in the basket and produce an amazing meal. Surprisingly, I cook the entire meal, with Jackie coaching me along. Now I know why she is such an amazing coach. If she can teach me, she can teach anyone. We put the chicken in the warmer, then Jackie leaves with a plate for Adaris and I hop in the shower.

***

As I head over to Keeva's house for what could literally be the "last supper," I decide to give Adaris a call.

"Hello."

"What's up, dude?"

"Waiting for my lovely to get back from giving your lady in waiting a cooking lesson."

"Oh, thank God! I can't tell you how thankful I am for Jackie. What are her favorite flowers—I want to send her a couple dozen tomorrow for helping keep me alive!"

"I am the only dude who's going to be sending her flowers, you home wrecker. And my baby doesn't really like flowers. She likes shoes and diamonds. But you can send me some flowers. I like roses."

"My bad Dair, I am not trying to break up your happy new home. Just tell me everything will be edible man!"

"You know that if my baby is in the kitchen, it will be delicious. Jackie is on her way home as we speak with a plate for your boy."

"Man, you are still outdoing me. I can't even eat until after you do!"

"Damn right. My wife knows how to take care of her man. You should pray that she is teaching Keeva a little something something about it. Gotta go. Mrs. Singleton has arrived with a hot plate of food," Adaris says, then he hangs up the phone.

All of a sudden I get a little nervous. Over the last eight months Keeva has never cooked for me. In fact, I don't recall Keeva ever inviting me over to her house before midnight.

One thing I do know is that this dinner is the beginning of something . . . well, something different, and very far from Keeva's normal routine. If I survive tonight I'll have a lot to think about. If not, I will be in Heaven!

***

I think about having a glass of wine to calm my nerves, but then I remember the last time I drank. Nope, I decide I need to have all of my faculties during this dinner. I already had to write down what Jackie told me to do: toss the potatoes, mash the chicken, and fry the salad. Oh, hell, that's not right!

As I turn around to grab my notes, the doorbell chimes, and I run to answer the door.

I fling it open and there stands Amos, larger than life and filling up my doorway. One thing I love about him is that he doesn't shy away from his hugeness. He embraces his girth in a way that is a total turn on. He leans down and kisses my cheek with those big lips, gives me a lazy smile, and says, "Are you going to let me in, beautiful, or make me stand out here all night?"

"That depends . . ."

"Depends?" he asks with a smirk.

"On what you plan to do to get invited in?" I say with a wink.

Amos leans down to eye level and says, "You obviously don't know me very well. I have always been the one to give you what you wanted, sometimes to my detriment. So what does it take, Keeva?"

"This conversation is getting way too deep. Come on in," I say, and I turn and walk down the hallway.

"You can run but you can't hide. Now, what's for dinner? I didn't eat all day in anticipation of this."

"I am afraid to ask—but in anticipation of what? I hope you aren't disappointed. I set the table in the dining room, so let me get you seated so I can serve you."

I lead Amos to a seat at the head of the table and drop a napkin on his lap. A girl doesn't want to get too close because it has been a few weeks, if you get my drift. Before I head back to the kitchen, Amos tugs on my arm and pulls me into his lap.

"Before you go I want to thank you for taking the time to set this beautiful table and cook for me. It's one of the nicest things you have ever done," he says, staring into my eyes.

"That's very sweet of you, but you're stalling, Amos."

"Yes I am, but I have missed holding you in my arms."

"Really? You're scared to eat my cooking aren't you?"

"Scared as hell, but I hope . . ."

"Hope what Amos?"

Amos lifts me up with one arm and reaches into his pocket with the other to get his phone out. He looks at it and beams.

"What is it?" I say, looking down at his phone.

Amos reaches over and gives me a kiss and says with his mouth still against my lips, "Since Adaris is still alive I guess I'll be ok."

I lean over, bite his bottom lip, and jump off his lap.

"Dammit Keeva, you bit me. That's not fair!" he yells.

"That's what you get for stalling until you got the high sign from Adaris. Blood obviously ain't thicker than water, you big wuss." That sets the playful mood for the evening.

I decide to bring all the food out at the same time so we can eat family style. Also because I can't remember what

127

should come first because in all the madness I have misplaced my notes. As much as I love to eat, I can't take my eyes off Amos. He's enjoying every morsel he puts in his mouth. No wonder Jackie convinced me to fry a whole chicken.

"Oh Keeva, this is so good! I can't believe you did this!"

"Me either. Jackie was a big help, but she made me do all the work while she talked me through it. I actually chopped, peeled, stirred, floured, and fried. And it was pretty cool."

"Well, you should definitely do it more often. With my fruit and vegetables and your cooking, we'd make a great team."

"Yeah, we would . . . I also have dessert."

"Dessert?" Amos says with a leer.

I jump up and come back with the warm blackberry cobbler, topped with vanilla ice cream.

"Oh Lord, I am a goner. The girl done made me some cobbler! Why don't we go sit on the couch and share a big bowl." Amos picks up a bowl and heaps a generous portion of cobbler and ice cream into it.

He grabs my hand, leads me over to the couch, then spreads his legs as he sits down and guides me to sit between them. When we've finished the last bite of the dessert, I lean back into Amos' chest and say, "This is nice. We really should do this more often."

Amos wraps his arms around my midriff and says, "It's so good to see you relaxing, baby." We just sit there, with no music and no words—just the sounds of the frogs and crickets singing their own little song in the Tennessee summer night.

I'm not sure how much time lapsed, but the next thing I know I'm waking from a doze to find Amos running his hands from the crown of my head to the base of my neck. Then he whispers in my ear how beautiful I look with my short haircut.

Suddenly I feel a vibration, and then I hear it. Still in my haze, I feel Amos pick me up, place me back on the couch, and cover me up with a blanket. I open my eyes and he leans over, kisses me gently on the lips, and says, "Thanks for dinner. It was delicious and so are you. I will let myself out."

Then he just walks out the door. I lie there on the couch, now wide awake. Wide awake and trying to figure out if I just dreamed that I made homemade salad dressing, peeled a bunch of potatoes, cut up a whole chicken and fried it up in a pan. I cannot believe that after all that Amos walks his monkey ass out the door for a booty call! I turn and look at the clock. It's 12:05 a.m.

I feel jilted! As I sit on my couch at 12:07, with the scent of Amos' cologne still on my body and the faint smell of fried chicken in the air, I try to imagine what my shrink Dominique would say. "Don't jump to conclusions. If you need clarity, just ask." Then I think about what Max would say. "Actions speak louder than words." Whoever sent that text to Amos is the reason why he left so abruptly which is why our intimate evening came to a screeching halt. Now, the old Keeva wants to pick up the damn phone and ask why he left me so abruptly, but the new Keeva decides to go to bed instead. All that cooking was exhausting, not to mention trying to maintain this new haircut. Now I know why people keep long hair or weaves.

So I get up, walk into my bedroom, and plop down on the left side of the bed—the 60 side. I turn over and notice that my cell phone is blinking. I pick it up and see that I have a text from Amos. "Thanks for a wonderful meal and even more wonderful company. Sweet dreams. Hunt." Before I can go into overthink mode, I put the phone down and go to sleep. I can overanalyze the text tomorrow.

***

I hated to leave Keeva. For the first time in I can't remember, we had a wonderful evening with no stressful moments. The meal was amazing, but more than that, Keeva seemed to really put her guard down and just relax. Honestly, the only other time I've seen her that vulnerable is in the bedroom. Just sitting there holding her and watching her sleep was awesome. That's why I knew I needed to leave before another day started. Staying would have led to intimacy, which would have been just more of the same. Keeva and I slept together after our third time hanging out, and believe it or not, she was the aggressor. If her loving wasn't so good I swear I would have felt violated. But she rocked my world. And since that date most of our time together has led to us getting down in the sheets. I soon learned that this is our comfort zone. I realize now that I really don't know much about Keeva. Yeah, I know she's a successful business woman and she loves her family and friends. But I've only seen her cry once, and that was when Jackie's team lost the sub-state playoff game. I want to get to know her outside the bedroom. I know that is the only way a relationship with her will survive.

So, I asked my boy World to send me a text message at 12:00 on the dot. That way if I was still at Keeva's house, I could get the hell out of dodge. World came through right on time, which is a good thing, because Keeva was smelling all good and feeling all good, and that could have led to a slumber party.

So I did what any coochie-whipped wimp would have done. I ran for my life before she could do or say something to convince me to stay. My boy Dair and Aunt D both warned me to act like a man. Keeva has already had enough boys in her life.

Adaris already talked about me bad enough on my way to Keeva's, so I decide to call World on my way home to get a pep talk.

"Yeah!" World growls into the phone.

"Hey man, I didn't wake you up, did I? I know you are a night owl."

"I'm a night owl, but my baby isn't. Make it quick, man. Max hasn't been feeling good and she just went to sleep."

"What's wrong with Max? Is she sick of you already?" I say with a chuckle.

"Not on your life. She was supposed to head back to St. Croix last week but she extended her stay. I'm trying to get her to take the New York bar exam and move here permanently. But you didn't call about that. What do you want, man?"

"Thanks for sending me the text. Your timing was perfect."

"This ain't Howard Johnson and I ain't going to keep being your wakeup call, so don't think I'm going to do this shit all the time. What was that about, anyway?"

"I had dinner at Keeva's tonight and I knew if I stayed past midnight I would be in deep trouble."

"What are you, Cinderella? Trouble as in knocking boots trouble?"

"Yeah man."

"So what's the problem with that?"

"The problem is that's the problem. I want her around indefinitely, and if I allow her to use me she will eventually get tired of me. That's her M.O."

"If she gets tired of you that means you're doing something wrong."

"Like make her sick, right?"

"Go to hell, you supersized punk. My baby has a virus."

"Yeah, a virus called World. Thanks again, Dog. I appreciate your support in my war for Keeva."

"Yeah, all right man. Just make sure you're prepared for a battle, because there's going to be hell to pay for walking out on Keeva's mean ass. Now get off my phone!"

***

World terminates the call, then turns over and kisses Max on her forehead. Max sleepily opens her eyes and says, "Is everything ok with Amos and Keeva, babe?"

World looks into the dark green eyes that first captivated him over a year ago He leans over to kiss her gently on the lips and says, "They're going to be just fine. I just had to give Hunt a pep talk. Go back to sleep."

Max closes her eyes and snuggles closer to World. He pulls her closer and snuggles his front against her back. Then he puts his hand over her stomach and gently kneads. As World closes his eyes, Max opens hers and silently prays, "Lord, I hope he doesn't sense what I think may be here in 34 weeks!

## Dair's Dare

I wake up Sunday morning to a text from Adaris:

*Greetns fam and frnds. Relay for Life rce for the cure is in 4 weeks! I need ur time — train to walk/run a 5k. Ur talent — recruit peple 2 run on the team n Ur treasure — yes I need ur $. The Mrs. and I have pledged $10k this yr in hnr of AJ and Coach Donovan.*

What the hell is he thinking sending a text like that at 7:00 in the morning? I wait a few hours and call Jackie.

"Morning sunshine!"

"What the hell are you and your husband up to with this Relay for Life crap?"

"We don't just want you to donate money this year, we want to get as many people as possible to join the bone marrow registry. Our goal is to recruit at least 100 people to donate $100 each, and add 100 donors to the registry."

"Can't I just write a check?"

"Of course you can, but we want 100 people to participate and we think we can do it."

"Ok, I'm in for one hundred bones, and tell Adaris I will do some pro-bono advertising for the event."

"Thanks girl, but we want you to actually participate."

"Oh no, boo, I don't run. I may walk a little, and if you need someone to hold the cup and give out water, I'm that girl."

"Amos said you wouldn't do it," says Jackie with a sad voice.

"Come again?"

"He said you wouldn't be a team player. Something about you being too bougie to break a sweat!"

"His country ass called me bougie! I'll have you know I have a black belt in karate, jiu jitsu, and tae kwon do! I can kick his ass three different ways, and you know I can keep up when you and I exercise together."

"That's Pilates and he also said you would brag about that. And that none of those sports involves breaking a sweat."

"Well, you and Amos can go to hell with all that reverse psychology crap. I'm going to run alright. In fact, you tell Amos Hunter that I will outrun his ass!"

"Keeva, you know Amos can run a 40-yard dash in 4.6 seconds, which is great for someone his size."

"I know all the stats, Jackie. Anyone can run that fast for 40 yards, but can he run an eight-minute mile?"

"Please Keeva. Don't push yourself to an eight-minute mile. You don't have enough time to train for that."

"Too late, it's on like popcorn, Jackie! I'm going to beat Amos like he stole something. Now, starting tomorrow you're going to meet me at the TSU track at 6:00 a.m. And don't be late!"

"You are an overachiever, Keeva. Be careful you don't bite off more than you can chew."

"I want to show him that there is more to me than beauty and brains."

"I would say that by the time the race gets here, you will have shown him you're not very smart, because this is one of the dumbest things you've done in a very long time. I'll see you tomorrow at seven, not six, and remember to dress light and bring lots of Gatorade."

***

### Day 1

The first day working out with Jackie is pure hell. She downloaded the "Couch to 5K" app and put me on the advanced plan—a nine-week program that needs to be shortened to four. I change my mind about her being a great coach. She is mean, she blows the whistle too damn much, and she is bossy. As I limp over to sit on the ground beside her, I look up at Jackie with a scowl and say, "I hate you and I am breaking up with you, you masochistic freak."

"Keeva, watch your language! You can't break up with your cousin. And you are the masochist. I just give the people what they want. Now we can stop . . . just say the word—"

"Hell no! I am in. I have 29 more days to go."

Jackie walks away laughing and calls back at me, "See you tomorrow at seven, you big cry baby."

"Forget you, Jackie!"

"I love you too, Keeva."

"Love you too. I'll call you later boo."

"Ok, girl."

For the first time in a long time I have taken on a challenge that I'm not sure I can accomplish, but I am going to get busy doing it, or die trying.


## Day 2

The next day I decide to piss Jackie off and be a little late. Actually, I'm so darn stiff and sore it takes me 20 minutes to get myself out the door. I arrive about ten minutes late, and as I limp onto the track I look around and am almost relieved to see that I have beat Jackie, until I see Amos on the ground stretching. Before I can say anything, he walks up to me and holds out a sealed envelope. I look up at him warily, yank it out of his hand, and rip it open.

*"Before you start cussing I want you to know I love you. Ok, I know that won't work. Adaris told me that Amos has more stamina than anyone on the team and he will be the best person to train you on day two. Someone else says keep your friends close and your enemies closer. Just don't sleep with the enemy. ☺ At least not today, because you are probably sore. Let Amos help get you in shape, girl. Again, I love you, and there's nothing you can do about it."*

I stand there for a minute and think about this whacked letter. And then I think about how my family told me to straighten up and fly right. I look up almost two feet at Amos and give him a sweet smile.

"Oh hell . . ."

"Oh hell what, Amos?"

"I meant, good morning. I'll be subbing for Jackie today. Something came up with Adaris and she couldn't make it."

"Oh, I bet something came up all right."

"What was that?"

"I said, aren't you a sight for sore eyes."

"Don't try to butter me up, girl. For the next two hours you are going to feel the pain. Now get stretched so we can get started."

As I limp off down the track I hear Amos say, "Keeva, watching you walk reminds me of the day after the first night we were intimate."

I whip around and before I can yell "ouch," I see that Amos is staring at me intensely. I say, "The only difference is that was a pleasure walk and this is painful."

"I will repeat the advice I gave you that day. Don't bite off more than you can chew."

"Well, one man's meat is another man's gravy," I say with a little pimp to my limp.

*Day 3*

The next day I decide at least to try to look a whole lot better than I'm feeling. Because who knows if Amos is going to show up. I climb slowly out of my car, then limp around the corner and see Leo standing on the track.

"What's up cuz, and what the hell are you wearing?"

*I am going to kill Jackie!!*

"What are you doing here Leo?"

"Jackie couldn't make it today, so I volunteered to sub for her before I go to class. By the way, there is no one out here, Keeva, so why are you dressed like that?"

"Would you stop looking at me like that? I feel like you are committing incest!"

"Well, technically, you're only my first cousin's cousin so we aren't really related—"

"But in real life you are my first cousin's brother, which makes you my first cousin, so step off!"

"Oh, I get it. You thought Amos was coming today and you decided to be all sexy and what not. So sorry you wasted your outfit. Now let's get started. We need to stretch, but let me turn my back because once you bend over, cousin or not, nothing will be left to the imagination."

*Day 4*

I walk around the corner, and before I see them I hear two very chipper people say, "Good morning, sunshine!"

"Yeah, yeah, Tiffany and Shelley. Tell me, to what do I owe the pleasure of you two love birds this morning?"

"We're a team, Keeva, and it takes a village to raise a— well, we really just had to see this," says Shelley. "And we wanted you to have some friendly trainers."

"Friendly my eye, Shelley. I heard about you. Amos told me you were the meanest captain on the team."

"The meanest, huh? Well good. That means I'm accomplishing my goal. Let's get started. Today you're going to run a lap and walk a lap, but we're going to pick up the pace just a little," he says, looking down at a sheet of paper.

"Are you looking at my stat sheet?"

"Yes, I am. Everyone has to report back to Jackie on your progress each day so she can adjust your workouts. You think *I'm* mean . . ." he says, shaking his head. "Tiff babe, I want you to time us."

"Why isn't she running?" I say, rolling my eyes at Tiffany.

Tiffany looks over at Shelley with a gleam in her eye and says, "I'll be walking with you but I can't run right now."

"Why not?"

"Because I finally knocked her up, and since we've been trying for so long I'm not gonna risk having her over exert herself, says Shelley with a Cheshire grin."

"Keeva, please don't say anything yet. I'm just starting my eighth week and we don't want to tell anyone until I'm in my second trimester," says Tiffany.

*What the heck is up with me and all my pregnant friends!*

"Just call me the baby whisperer," I mutter under my breath.

"What did you say?" says Shelley.

"I said, way to go mister, and you too Tiffany. But as for keeping your little secret, I should at least get to be a god-auntie or something. Now let's get this party started, shall we?"

"Yep, someone told me you were trying to run an eight-minute mile. Which means we need to try to run a lap in two minutes. Keeva, are you sure—"

"I know it's damn near impossible, but let's shoot for the stars, even if we have to settle for the moon."

"That's my girl. You ready to time us Tiff?"

### *Day 5*

By day five I'm about ready to pull out what little nappy hair I have left. I have no idea who will meet me at the track this morning. I called Jackie the night before, but she immediately put me in my place.

"Keeva, you were the one who said you were going to keep up with Amos. If you go back on your word I will never let you live it down," says Jackie.

"But you didn't tell me Fat Albert and the gang would be training me!"

"When I told everyone you were running, I got a bunch of volunteers to help you get in shape. All except-"

"Except who, Jackie?"

"Well . . . Amos wasn't too excited about you running—"

"Why not! It's not the 'Amos Hunter' race, it's the Relay for Life. You get a message to him girly!"

"And what would that message be, cousin?"

"Getting formal on me, ain't you cuz? You tell him that he ain't running nothing but his mouth and that in 26 days his big ass is grass," I say, slamming down the phone.

***

Jackie gently hits "end" on her phone, turns and grins at Adaris and Amos. "She took the bait," she says, grinning. "Now what Amos?"

"By the time I get done with her, not only will she be in great shape but she will be eating out of my hand."

"You just better hope she doesn't eat you alive, man. Believe me, the women in this family are man eaters," says Adaris, shaking his head.

"I can't get her on the turf, but if I can get her to let down her guard and make herself vulnerable, we may stand a chance. How else can I get her with no phone, no makeup, and, according to Leo's report, no clothes. I need her to be unencumbered, and if that means torturing everyone in the process to help me strip Keeva down to her essence, then we will do it together or all die trying!"

Adaris leans toward Amos and says, "If I didn't know you were a little emotional about winning your girl I would kick your ass for yelling at my wife, but I'll give you a pass this one time. You feel me, Hunt?"

"Sorry for being so emotional Jackie. Day six will be a big surprise. I figure we can let those two drive her nuts. And I think I'll take day seven. That's your favorite number, isn't it Adaris?" Amos says, while back pedaling out of the room.

***

Who knows what I will run into on my fifth day of torture. My give-a-shit factor is way down, so I figure whoever today's coach is will feel the wrath of Keeva. I walk around the corner to the track and start looking around, but I don't see anyone. Thank God. Maybe today I can work out in peace . . . or maybe not work out at all. Just as I'm about to walk off the track I hear a phone ringing. Of course I'm too nosey not to investigate, so I walk close to the phone and see a note that says, "Answer the phone you freak!" Now I am obviously too intrigued to be offended by the nasty little note, so I do what any self-respecting freak would do . . . I answer the phone.

"Hello."

"Good morning!"

"Who the hell is this?"

"You know who this is, girl. It's me, Max."

"And I am on the phone too, Keeva," yells Chris in the background.

Now anyone else would have thrown the phone down and run like the wind, but I am obviously a glutton for punishment because I stand there with my mouth open.

"Close your mouth, Keeva. It's mosquito season down there in Tennessee. You had to know that Chris and I would want to get in on this little training session. Now, I want you to hang up the phone, and then we're gonna Facetime you."

Like a robot I follow Max's instructions wondering how she knew my mouth was open and then all of a sudden I see her ugly face and Chris's beautiful face right beside her.

"What the hell do the two of you want?"

"You know what we want. When we heard about the little training program Jackie put together for you, we told her we wanted in," says Max.

"You know all I need to do is hang up this damn phone, don't you Max?"

"You can hang it up if you want, but if you do you will never hear the end of it Keeva."

"Move out of the way, ugly. If I have to spend the time with the two of you I want to look at Chris."

"Hey little bit. Today we're going to work on your breathing while you run. I am actually going to run with you, but on a treadmill. Walk around the stadium and you'll see a treadmill ready for you to jump on."

"Are you kidding me? You actually went to all this trouble? I take back everything I ever said about you. But where is your treadmill Max?" I say with a raised eyebrow and a smirk.

"I'm not running today Keev. I've been having some stomach issues so I'll just help Chris keep track of your breathing."

"Oh . . . so this is kind of like a Lamaze class, huh Max?"

I almost regret my bad behavior, but that's what Max's ass gets for making fun of me. I also want to remind her that I haven't forgotten about her little secret. After a small shuffle, the phone is handed over to Chris.

"Cat got your tongue, Max?"

"Ok baby girl, let's get started. Max had to run to the bathroom. We are going to start the warm up with the speed on 2.5 and gradually get up to about 5. You ready to pick 'em up and put 'em down?"

"What the hell is pick 'em up and put 'em down?"

"It's what you are going to do with those pretty legs of yours today. That's all you need to focus on for the next hour. You ready?" says Chris.

"Yeah, I guess Chris." And so it went. An hour workout via Facetime. As we begin our cool down, Chris has to step away to talk to his agent, which leaves me alone with Max.

"All right Max. Now that I have you to myself, what is going on with you girl?"

"Nothing girl. Just hanging out with Chris for the summer."

"So . . . have you been to the doctor yet?"

"Not yet, but I am going soon to find out what is going on with my stomach."

"If you don't go soon it is going to be quite apparent what is going on. Don't let Chris find out about this without you telling him, Max."

"I hear you girl. I just don't know what I want to do at this point."

"What do you mean, you don't know? Like, whether you'll stay in New York or go back to St. Croix know what to do?"

"I wish it were that simple . . . I mean, like if I should keep it or not."

"Oh Max. We are way too old to be contemplating keeping a child versus aborting one. Don't you love Chris?"

"Yes, I love him Keeva, but we have a lot of issues, which includes living in two different places. He just went through a very nasty divorce and has mentioned more than once that he isn't ready to have a family. And I honestly don't want to raise a child by myself or have a baby daddy!"

"But he loves you, Max. People change their minds very quickly when a child comes into play. You won't know if you don't talk to him about it."

"Before I talk to him about it, let me get confirmation from a doctor."

"All right girl. I'll stop pestering you but I sure hope the shit doesn't hit the fan."

"The what? You people say the dumbest things . . ."

"What people would you be referring to Max?"

"Obviously not black people, since I am also one of you. I mean you country ass Tennessee people."

### Day 6

At this point I've learned to expect the unexpected, and as I walk around the corner of the track I see Nashville's finest. Well, Nashville's youngest finest. Yes, it appears to be most of Seymour High School's basketball team, sans Jackie but including AJ's younger brother Noah, Jackie's not-really stepson.

"To what do I owe the pleasure fellas?"

"Good morning, Ms. Keeva. We heard that you were working on getting tight and right for the race, and we told Coach Jackie we would be happy to assist in getting you in shape," says Scoop.

As Scoop is talking, about ten teenage boys surround me in a circle. "You haven't left for Rollins College yet Scoop?" I ask, glaring at the others who look like they're waiting on his permission to speak.

"Naw Shorty. Your boy doesn't leave until August. And don't try to get us off task by changing the subject."

"Yeah, Coach Jackie warned us that you would try it, but we ain't biting," says Peaches.

AJ, who is one of the few boys with good sense and manners, steps up, wraps his arm around me, and says, "Aunt Keeva, thanks for sacrificing your time to get ready for this race. It means a lot to me and I know to Coach Donovan. I am going to stay with you the entire run today. The rest of these jokers are going to do sprints and hills," he says, jerking his head toward the rest of the squad.

"And I am going to run right behind you, Ms. Keeva to make sure you have the correct form," says Noah with a smirk.

"Really Noah? 'Cause I have a feeling you're supposed to be doing what the rest of the team is doing, you little per—"

"Yeah, little brother. Now is not the time to try to hit on Aunt Keeva. We only have three weeks left before the race," says AJ.

AJ and I walk onto the field and start to stretch. Peaches leans over and says, "You sure are looking good this morning Keeva, even without makeup."

"Well I—"

"I got this Aunt Keeva. Peaches man, you know you don't need to be trying to step to my aunt like that."

"I heard she is free game since she and Amos aren't talking any more."

*Who told him that?!*

"Well, what would make you think she would want you, Peaches?"

By this time I'm starting to get a little tired of all of these infants talking about me like I'm not here, so I jump in and say, "Well, I may be a little older—"

"I got this, Aunt Keeva," AJ says again, now narrowing his eyes at Peaches.

"Well, I am good looking and she's fine and we are both available, and you know I am over age 18 now, right Keeva baby?" the little wimp says while pretending to pop his collar.

AJ, who is well over six feet tall, jumps up from the ground and starts moving toward Peaches. Hell, this is the most excitement I've had in a long time! Two men fighting over me—well, two boys. So I lean back to watch the show.

"Peaches, my man, I have been wanting to tell you this for a long time, and today is the perfect time. Just because someone is fine and available does not mean they want you."

*I knew I loved that boy for some reason.*

"You see, it takes more than looks and some mindless flirting to win a woman over," says AJ.

*You tell him baby boy!*

"So you say. Well, it's worked for me for this long, so why not get a little practice in today?"

*Practice? Do I need to get up and ring his little short scrawny neck?* Before I can get up, AJ steps closer to Peaches.

"I got this, Aunt Keeva. Why not is because my aunt is too old, too mature, and too smart to give you the time of day," says AJ, getting up in Peaches' face.

*He is doing pretty well, except the "too old part."*

"And furthermore, my brother, I need you to start respecting your elders. She is Ms. Keeva or Ms. McGhee to you from now on. And on another note, you need to stop pushing up on Sophia."

*Oh . . . so that's what this is all about. It's always about a chick, ain't it?*

"Dude, Sophia and I were doing fine until your punk ass came along," says Peaches.

By now the two boys are toe to toe, but AJ has Peaches by about six inches and 50 pounds. I really want to step in, but I haven't seen a good fight since Jackie threw up on Adaris last year, and this is getting good.

"Peaches, you may call yourself a man, but only a boy would keep pushing up on someone who isn't interested. And

150

if you think Sophia is rough, you should see Aunt Keeva in action. She is brutal. She will chew you up and spit you out."

*What! Am I really that bad?*

"Learn to read the signs playa. Sophia doesn't want you, and neither does Aunt Keeva." AJ takes a deep breath, steps around Peaches, but not without brushing his shoulder against his chest. Then he bends down to lift me up. And that boy-man is strong—he lifts me up with no effort. Now I can see how his father charmed the shorts off Jackie!

"Come on Aunt Keeva. Let's get this run in right quick. Now, Peaches, I know you are no longer on my team, but we would love for you to work out with us until you leave for the Navy. But, it's a new day, so we do it my way. You feel me?"

"Yeah man, I feel ya."

With that the boy-man and the man-boy give each other a pound, then AJ and I take off on a slow jog while Peaches goes back to join the team that he is no longer a part of. As we run lap after lap around the track I realize a lot of things. Picking and choosing your battles at the right time is crucial, and sometimes words out of the mouth of babes is priceless. But most important, I've started to see that fighting fair is empowering. And then it really hits me. All week God has put all these people in my path for a very obvious reason. They aren't just coming out here to teach me how to stretch, breath, and pace myself. They are here to teach me some valuable lessons. And this big young man who has been quietly encouraging me the entire time we've been running is truly his father's child. I realize how blessed and fortunate my sister-cousin Jackie is to have him and his father in her life.

As we finish our cool down I look over at AJ and say, "Thanks for today. It means more to me than you will ever know."

"I am honored that Coach Mama Jackie allowed me to help out, Aunt Keeva. And I am so proud of you."

"No young man. I am proud of you. You give me hope."

### Day 7

I swear by day seven I have had enough. Enough of Jackie and her couch to 5K idea. Enough of being sore, and enough of waking up at the butt crack of dawn. Enough of this workout crap and sweating out my hair, and enough of being a damn nervous wreck because I have no idea who will be coming to train me. And Jackie is not answering her phone— she just sends me a text each night and says "see you tomorrow." Well, mañana has gotten on my damn nerves. I have three more weeks before the event and I'll be damned if I'm going to quit.

I get up on Sunday morning, throw on some raggedy shorts and a T-shirt with a hole in the armpit, slip into my most comfortable tennis shoes, and go to the track. I don't care who comes this morning. All I want to do is have a good stretch and get through this workout, and then go home. As I walk around the corner I spot Amos leaning back against the bleachers. If I didn't think it would just make me feel worse, I'd have a two-year-old type tantrum. That is, before I kill Jackie! Here I am looking all jacked up and there he is looking juicy fruity and good and what not. Then I remember why people say there is a thin line between love and hate, I both hate and love that he is here. Then I think about Uncle Shorty and decide to put my game face on. I walk up to Amos as sexy as I can be in my state of dress and say, "I see you made it here right after the strip clubs closed. And I just bet you don't have any money left."

"Good morning to you, Keeva. You don't have to take your anger out on me because you're up so early. I actually called Jackie to see if I could be your workout partner this morning so we can start the beginning of our week together." Then he leans down to give me a kiss on the cheek.

"Hmm . . . well that was nice of you, Amos. I actually thought you were here to taunt me like everyone else this week."

"Most people don't make it to day seven, and believe it or not, if you make it through today exercising will become a habit for you."

"To be honest, I've wanted to quit every day. But I am starting to like the way I feel. At least the way I feel toward the middle of the day. My blood pressure is down and I've been sleeping better."

"It's good to know something else can put you to sleep besides me! But seriously, exercise is good for the mind and the body. It's also something we can do together. Now come on, let's get you stretched so you can stop walking like a zombie. Today I'm going to teach you how to be kinder to your feet. You are very flat and heavy footed, I can show you a technique that will take some pressure off your back and feet. Now, let's get you warmed up."

Amos leads me through a round of stretches that help me loosen up, then we begin our workout. Before I know it we have finished and are starting our cool down.

"I never actually thought I would enjoy exercising, but today has been . . . well, I can't describe it."

"Some would say you finally got your second wind. Kind of like an athlete's or runner's high. Or in layman's terms you're starting to get to where exercising is no longer painful. Most people don't make it that far before they quit."

"This is almost orgasmic!"

"Yes, which is why it was so important for me to be here today." Amos gives me a wink.

I smile back at him. "Well, Amos, thanks for helping me pop my runner's cherry."

"It was my pleasure Keeva!"

# A Line in the Sand

When I started this running journey four weeks ago, I had no idea what changes I would see in my mind and body. My stress level is down, and according to everyone associated with me I am much nicer to be around. I realize that letting go of all—make that most—of my emotional baggage has been very good for me and also opened my eyes to so many things around me. All of my hard work is about to culminate in a race to honor one man whom I adored and who left a legacy with all 171 people on our team. But it also helped me appreciate how far AJ has come since he became a cancer survivor.

Tonight Aunt Ella is hosting a pre-race dinner at the Plantation that'll include lots of carbs to help the run/walkers get ready for tomorrow. This will be an intimate gathering—we'll get together tomorrow with the much larger group. All of my girls will of course be on the scene. The last time we've all been together was at Jackie's wedding reception.

Today is the first time in over three weeks that I'll see Amos, so I decide to wear something that will leave him feeling some kind of way. Hell, the last few times he has seen me I looked like death warmed over so I have nowhere to go but up! Who knows . . . I got lucky the last time we were at Aunt Ella's house—he felt me up in the most marvelous way. I have always admired my legs, and over the last month they've become even more nicely defined. I am feeling tantalizing and I can't wait for everyone to see me. My outfit for the night is a pair of high-waisted shorts and a sleeveless peplum top, finished off with four-inch espadrilles. My hair has been fried, died, and laid to the side, which was a total waste of money since I'm gonna sweat it out tomorrow during the race. Oh, the things we do for lust! And to think that a few months ago I was giving Jackie the business for dressing up to impress a man.

I pull up at Aunt Ella's house with my paper plates, cups, and napkins—the same thing I always bring. But I decided to surprise them by bringing a Greek salad to go with the pasta.

Before I can open the door it swings open to Serena, Max, and Jackie, who are standing side by side smiling down at me. No matter what the three of them do or where we are, I am excited to see them. They are the peanut butter to my jelly, the salt to my pepper, the French fries to my burger. I just love these three broads.

"Keeva girl, you are glowing! Exercise looks good on you," says Serena.

"I agree with Rena. Who knew a dare from Amos could elevate Keeva's beauty. Girl, you look good," says Max.

The girls surround me and give me a big group hug.

"I am proud of you Keeva. I know the last month has been tough, but I knew you could do it," says Jackie. "You are

157

mentally the toughest of all of us. Dad always told me I needed a little more of you in me, Keeva."

"Uncle Shorty said that?" I say as tears well up in my eyes.

"Stop crying Keeva. And yes, Daddy told us all the time that the thing he loved the most about you was your resolve to succeed no matter what. After Aunt Jean died you finished college, you pushed forward after Damian, and you've created a wonderfully successful business. It takes a lot of grit to pick up the pieces and keep moving. This little 5k is nothing compared to all that," says Serena.

"Leave it to you Rena to give me this little rallying cry after the fact! I needed that pep talk crap a month ago."

"No you didn't chica. You weren't ready a month ago. You were pissed and horny and that is where you needed to be. We wanted you to stay confused and off balance, and it worked," says Jackie.

"And if we had told you this back then you'd have gotten the big head and quit," says Max.

"You needed a challenge, girl. You were getting bored, and we know what happens when Keeva gets bored. All hell breaks loose," says Serena with a chuckle.

"To sum it all up, don't let yourself get too comfortable, Keeva. Now prance into the kitchen, load up on some carbs, sleep tight, and get your mind right," says Jackie.

"Oh hell, I knew this little celebration wouldn't last long. Coach Jackie and her little minions are back," says Keeva.

"I am nobody's minion. I speak for myself, but I agree with you little sis," says Serena.

"I concur as well," says Max.

As the posse heads to the kitchen, I lean over to Max and say, "Tonight is all about me but tomorrow it's on like Donkey Kong Maxine. I need some answers."

You know how women can talk. After everyone finishes roasting me about my lack of dating skills, we move on to the usual topics, like when Jackie is going to have her first baby, if Serena will have another baby, and Aunt Ella's potential new baby, which she evades smoothly, like butter. I swear those Donovan women know how to not answer a question.

And as usual I get clean-up duty cause in our family, those who cook don't clean. But since my successful cooking lesson I've been finding out that cooking and cleaning aren't so bad. Knowing that most of the guests will be walking or running in the morning, we decide to make this an early night.

I notice that Aunt Ella is fixing coffee. "Aunt Ella, we aren't supposed to be drinking caffeine this close to a race."

"Who told you that, niece?"

"Jackie told me that, didn't you Jackie?" I notice that Serena's ass as usual is poking out from the refrigerator and it is shaking.

"What the hell is so funny this time? You broads are always laughing at my expense!"

Serena turns around, closes the fridge, and tells me, "You can't believe everything that Jackie tells you Keeva. She probably just told you that because you were already bouncing off the walls."

"Don't pay those girls any mind, Keeva. It's not the best idea to drink caffeine because you are already anxious enough about any major event and it just gives you another reason not to relax. But, I'm not running tomorrow honey."

"And you prefer tea, so who are you making coffee for?"

"No wonder you struggle so much in the dating arena. Not only are you mean but you are slow," says Serena.

"Even I figured this one out," says Max.

"Well, would someone please hip me to the game!"

"It appears that mom is having a nightcap after we all make our exit," says Serena.

"I taught my sister well. And with that I will take my leave," says Aunt D.

By the time I finally figure out what is going on, the men come in from outside. As I watch Micah and Jordan escort Rena out and Adaris grab Jackie's hand to give it a gentle kiss, it hits me again that the love boat is sailing on without me. Shelley gently rubs Tiffany's stomach, and then I sense a shadow looming over me.

"Come on Keeva, let's head out so I can get you ready to run tomorrow," Amos whispers in my ear.

"Head out?" I say, feeling confused. In fact, I feel like someone slipped me a mickey.

"Yes, you're staying at my place tonight. Dair and Jackie asked us to have an accountability partner so we can make sure we get downtown on time in the morning."

"So did you get the short straw and end up with me?"

"No, little bit, I actually chose you. Leave your car here and you can get it tomorrow after the celebratory cookout."

"But I don't have any of my clothes, or toiletries, and I—"

"I got you baby, now let's be out. Say goodnight to everyone."

"Goodnight to everyone."

Amos grabs my hand and walks me out to his Hummer before I can fully figure out what is going on. He picks me up and places me gently in the seat, then buckles my seatbelt. As we pull out of the driveway, I start coming to my senses and the questions begin.

"Now tell me again why I'm not going home?"

"Because you are coming home with me," says Amos with a smile.

"And why aren't we going to my house?"

"Because mine is closer and my bed is bigger."

"Of course it is. You're 6 feet 7. But I just got a new Sleep Number mattress, and besides, you usually come to my house."

"Well, we are going to change things up a bit."

"Why?"

"Because I say so Keeva. For once in your life will you stop questioning every little thing and just be."

"Just be what?"

"Just be quiet! Now, I'm going to put on that Norman Brown cd you love so much, so sit back and relax, and sip on this water so we can make sure you're hydrated tomorrow."

And, well, there is nothing else to say. So I sit back in the seat, which is surprisingly comfortable for a war vehicle, sip my water, hum along with my baby Norman, and "just be." It is the most peaceful I have felt in a long time.

I swear there is something in the water, because the next thing I know I'm lying on top of Amos on his huge bed wearing pajamas. I bury my head in his chest and say, "Amos—"

"Remember Keeva, just be. Its 1:00 in the morning, you are in my bed, and I want you to get a good night's sleep. You have a big run in the morning."

I don't really know what happened after that, but I do remember feeling Amos' lips settle on mine, and the next thing I know he's shaking me awake.

"Good morning. Your shower is running and your clothes are in the bathroom. You have 30 minutes. When you're done come in the kitchen for breakfast."

I look up at a smiling Amos who is fully dressed in a navy blue jogging suit with massive running shoes on his boat-like feet.

I head to the bathroom in a sleepy stupor. How I got from Aunt Ella's and ended up in a humongous bed draped across Amos in a blissful sleep I will never know. I look down and see that I'm wearing some cute pajamas with a top and boy shorts. I slowly peel them off and step into the huge walk-in shower that has about ten showerheads on the back wall. This shower is big enough to fit ten people Amos' size or bigger. I just stand there letting all the jets hit me from every direction. I eventually remember that I'm supposed to be running a 5k in a few hours, and after giving myself something between a pep talk and a brow beating, I step out of the shower and towel off.

I look over at the counter and see a blue and white running outfit with matching running shoes. What is it with these Trailblazers? Hell, they don't need to play football, they need to start a fashion line for women. I recall the countless times Adaris dressed Jackie during their courtship.

I figure, what the heck, I don't have anything else to wear. As I bend over to put my shoes on, I feel Amos over me again.

"What is with you being so big but walking like a gazelle? I never hear you coming!"

"That's funny, because I can feel and hear you stomping a mile away," says Amos, bending over to be at eye level with me.

"My shrink says that's all part of my Napoleon complex. Aunt Ella says all the women in our family are heavy walkers."

"The reason I walk so quiet is because my high school coach made me take a ballet class to improve my balance and agility. Now, let's get your shoes on so we can get going." Amos picks up my heavy size six feet, pulls my socks on and double knots my shoes. I swear it is the sexiest thing he has ever done.

I have to do something to get back on track, so I gently punch his shoulder and say, "I can put my own shoes on Amos."

"I know, but it's an honor to bow at your feet."

"I thought World was the one with the foot fetish. Now I know why Max is . . . "

"You know why Max is what?"

"So addicted to Chris. Are you going to feed me before you throw me to the wolves, Amos?"

"You bet your tighter ass I am going to feed you, but I am the only wolf you need to worry about. This run is to support your family, it's not a competition, Keeva."

"Oh yes it is. I am going to finish this race, Amos. I finally realized there is no way I can beat you, but since I've trained for over a month I am determined to finish."

"I will be with you all the way. Let's just take one mile at a time."

We arrive at the run/walk venue, and Amos walks off to get us registered. I head off to find Jackie and the rest of the group.

"Hey cuz, I thought you were going to fink out on me when you left with Amos last night."

"You know I am not a fink out kind of girl. What the hell are you laughing at?"

"Turn around Keeva!"

As I turn around, Jackie starts laughing even harder.

"I see I am still the butt of your damn jokes. What the hell is so funny?"

"I am laughing because you obviously let Amos dress you!"

"Well, yes, he dressed me because I didn't get a chance to go home and get any clothes, which I am sure you had something to do with!"

"Did you pay any attention to the outfit, or did you dress in the dark?"

"Well . . . actually I did dress in the damn dark. What is it?"

"Well, for one he put you in some runner's shorts. Thank goodness you have no ass at all, but you are working those legs girl. So I guess you didn't see the back of your shirt, right?"

"No, you Amazon. Now out with it before I kick you in the shin!"

"The back of your shirt says, 'The Hunted.'"

"The what? No wonder he rocked me to sleep, put me in that big ass shower, tied my shoes, and fed me. He was trying to distract me! It almost worked. He actually had me getting all soft and shit. He better be glad I am not as flat in the boob area as I am in the butt area or I would take off this shirt and throw it in his face," I say.

As I stomp off in search of Amos, I remember what Amos said about me stomping and I soften my steps to a strut. As I get closer to our team I see Amos talking to Jazzmine. I squint my eyes to get a better look, and Amos looks up and gives me a big smile. I look at him, give him my most devious smile, raise my right hand and blow him a kiss, and then I turn around and put my hand on my flat ass and walk away.

"Amos, it looks like you just pissed off your girl. I thought you were making headway with Keeva," says Jazzmine, rubbing Amos' shoulder."

"Two steps forward and three steps back, at least in Keeva's mind. She must have found out what I put on the back of her shirt.

"Not to mention, she probably thinks you and I have something going on. I hope she realizes that things aren't what they may seem."

***

"All right everyone, time to head to the starting line. Those who plan to run, please make your way toward the front and get ready for the starting gun."

"Keeva, are you ready to get started? I would suggest we line up toward the middle so we can set a good pace," says Amos.

"With the stunt you just pulled you have drawn a line in the sand."

"The T-shirt was just a little joke, baby. You aren't mad are you? My shirt says 'The Hunter.' You get it, Hunter, Hunted? It's just a play on my name."

"I got it, smart ass. Now why don't you go back there with your little friend while I do what you dared me to do four weeks ago?"

The gun goes off, and in my rage I take off running. At the half mile mark I start to pick up the pace, and I hear Amos say, "Babe, you are running too fast. Slow down some so you can make it through the race."

I huff out, "Shut up Amos!"

"Breathe through your nose."

"Leave me alone Amos." Which he does, until . . .

"Pick up your feet baby!"

I spin around with the little energy I have left and whisper, "Leave me alone Amos . . ."

"Keeva, baby, you can't stop in the middle of the street. You have about a mile to go. Come on, get your second wind. You can finish!"

"I can't do this Amos. You win, you beat me."

"You can finish. This isn't about beating each other. It's about accomplishing a goal. Now come on. I'm right here and we'll finish together."

"But—"

"Just be, Keeva. Stop talking and concentrate on breathing. You can cuss me out later."

I don't finish the 5k in 40 minutes, it's more like an hour and ten, but at least I finish. And when I do I realize that a 5k isn't five miles . . . it's more like three miles and some change! I almost fall flat on my face at the finish line, but Amos catches me. Then he swings me up, tosses me over onto his back, and gives me a piggy back ride. If I weren't so damn tired I'd admire the view from almost seven feet up, lick out my tongue at Jazzmine, flip a bird at Jackie and thump Amos on the back of the head in that order. But I can only find the strength to mumble, "Thank you for believing in me Amos."

"I always knew you could do whatever you put your mind to, Keeva. I am so proud of you—now you need to believe in yourself," he says, swinging me around to cradle me like a baby against his chest. He moves his hands down to cradle my flat butt and gives me a sweaty kiss.

"Where are you taking me now, Amos?"

"We'll head back to my house so you can shower and rest. I'm heading over to Ms. Ella's house to help with the grilling for the party. Your car is parked at my house, so you can head over once you get dressed."

"How did my car get from Aunt Ella's to your house?"

"Don't worry about it Keeva. Just let me take care of you sometimes."

"Speaking of taking care, why don't we head to your house and—"

"Believe me, you don't have the strength to even think about that. You will rest alone. Any temporary pleasure is not worth me losing the long-term gain."

"What does that mean, Amos?"

"It means that I am not going to dumb myself down, pimp myself out, or chase some tail. If I do, we both lose."

"So are we really just playing a game?"

"I am playing the most important game of my life, and I'm trying to make sure you're on my team. Let's do it my way, Keeva. We'll both know when it's time to sleep together again, but we need to be sure we're on the same page. Believe me, if we can re-create the synergy we have had in the past, imagine what it could be like in the future."

"You can't resist me Amos, and you know it."

"I never said I could, baby. You are the sweetest thing I have ever known." And with that he kisses me on my collarbone.

# Keep It in the Closet

I haven't heard from Amos since the night of the race and I'm starting to feel some kind of way, but I'm determined not to call him. I got a call from Adaris regarding some training Game Changers is hosting for the Tennessee Trailblazers. From what he said, a lot of the players are ill equipped to do anything other than play football. Because they're such great athletes, these men tend to overlook a lot of things they really needed to know—like how to read above a third-grade level and balance a checkbook, let alone manage their own financial affairs. You don't find many athletes like Magic Johnson, Shaquille O'Neal, and Adaris Singleton, who were not only students of their games but also of their paychecks. I'm looking forward to helping Adaris and Chris realize their dream of creating financial independence for as many athletes that will listen. To be honest, I'm tired of hearing the horror stories of famous athletes who have to sell their championship rings and trophies just to make ends meet.

But I'm torn about coming to this meeting today. If not for Amos being in the room I would be just fine, but I'm not sure I'm ready to see him. Last week he had me feeling all gushy and loved and tender. He did things to me that no other man has done, and it wasn't the slap it up flip it rub it down oh no kind of feeling. It was the everlasting love kind of feeling. The love will conquer all kind of thing.

So I decide, if the mountain won't come to Muhammad then Muhammad must go to the mountain, and I am coming with guns a-blazing. Since I've become a bit of a runner, the guns I am talking about are my killer legs and arms. I decide to wear a red sleeveless dress that stops at the knee. Yes, the dress has a jacket, but I decided to leave it at home. I pair it with black 6-inch stilettos. If I don't feel powerful I can at least look like I do. I also decide to spike my hair and keep the makeup minimal—just powder, mascara, and bright red lipstick. There are a lot of good looking, athletic, wealthy men coming to this meeting, and I plan to do some ego building today.

I decide to meet Jackie at the stadium. I don't think I can take too much of her happiness. Since she and Adaris got married, I, actually, since they met she has been floating on cloud nine. While I'm happy about her marital bliss, I'm not so happy about the state of my affairs—or, rather, lack thereof. I haven't felt this restless in a long time, and what really pisses me off is that I can't explain why I feel this way. Here I am a 30-something single woman with a great career, more money in my checking account than I have ever had, a beautiful car and house, and none of that is making me happy. Not even the new Chanel purse I'm rocking on my right shoulder. Yes, I have it all. At least what the world would say is "it all." But I really don't have a damn thing because the guy I am gunning for is here in this man-sized conference room, and there is nothing I can do about it. Maybe this is what Uncle Shorty meant when he said that you could learn two the hard way. In this instance, "two the hard way" means I played with fire and now it has been extinguished.

As I'm walking toward the stadium I hear a really loud whistle. It can't be anyone other than Jackie. For someone so refined, she can be really ghetto. I slowly turn around, and there she is in all of her 6-foot-2 loveliness. She is glowing in a beautiful black pantsuit and some amazing shoes. How a woman who is already 5 foot 11 can wear four-inch heels is beyond me.

"Dang cuz, you are taking power to a whole new level, aren't you? You got the Olivia Pope thing working like a mother. All you need are some gloves."

"I had to do something, girl. Wearing red is the only way Amos is going to notice me today. It's been over a week since the run and I haven't heard a word from him."

"What's wrong with your phone, Keeva? If you really want to talk to Amos, why don't you call him? The days when you had to wait for a man to call are long gone. And you are the most untraditional person I know."

"Call him and say what, Jackie? My heart is yearning for your love?"

"Well, is your heart yearning for his love? 'Cause if it is you should tell him that. But don't sing it. You have a lot of talent but that gift passed over you. And I love The Gap Band too much to hear you desecrate that song."

"Stop trying to change the subject. You took Adaris up on this offer primarily so you can see Amos without him thinking you are trying to see him. I hope you don't think you're fooling anyone, Keeva. Amos is smarter than you give him credit for. You have to know that he is being just as crafty as you think you are trying to be."

"Crafty. My, isn't that a word from the English major. You should come up with something better than that, like cunning, deceptive, or malicious."

"Did you take your meds this morning Keeva? I need you to be firing on all pistons with this group."

"I am not taking any meds, and you are irritating me Jackie. Like when someone says 'leave a brief but detailed message' irritating."

"Irritating you or pissing you off?" Jackie says with a laugh. "You are one big fat oxymoron today Keeva. Why don't you really tell me what has your panties in a wad?"

"You hit the nail on the head. What has my panties in a wad is absolutely nothing!"

"English, Keeva. I don't understand you."

"Amos has not tried to sleep with me once since he almost seduced me in Aunt Ella's basement."

"Nothing, Keeva?"

"Oh, that forehead kiss shit and a piggy back ride and a gallant move of putting my shoes on, but that's it."

"Sounds like he's courting you, Keeva. I know you have no idea what that means, but I believe it's working."

"What do you mean, you moron?"

"Watch your language. I know you and Max call each other names, but I am still tall enough to step on you. What I am saying is, embrace the difference, Keeva. You have been Ms. 'We are the world' for so long that you have forgotten about home. I must admit I was a little inebriated the day you and Amos met, but I could still see that he had you intrigued."

"You were a whole lot drunk, and sick and rude. But I digress. Because I liked your swagger. He did have me a little scared by his sheer size and I did like that he was country smart, but he did not move the crowd the first time I met him. He actually got on my damn nerves talking in third person."

"But he was different from all the others, Keeva."

"By different you must mean he was more aggravating!"

"Stop acting like you are stuck on stupid. You know that boy rocked your world."

"He may have tilted it a little, Jackie, but I am getting sick and tired of playing these mind games. Ain't nobody got time for that!"

"Mind games . . . it seems to me as if you have fallen and bumped that big head of yours. Just in case you don't recall, you are the one who played all the games. You have that boy's nose so wide open he can't even see straight. But you best believe that he has his game face on now, so you better watch your back!"

*** 

Upstairs in the conference room, Adaris, Shelley, and Amos are in a huddle of their own.

"Why do you keep pacing, Hunt? You're gonna wear out the carpet, man."

"You know why. I haven't seen Keeva in days, and I have no idea how she'll react when she sees me today," says Amos.

"The women in the Donovan family know how to turn it on and off. Ms. Ella and Aunt D have taught them well."

"That's what I am afraid of, Shelley. Keeva is used to getting her way, and my time may be up."

"Now is not the time to panic, Hunt. Get it together. If Keeva sees a crack in your exterior she will walk all over you. I know we are in the stadium, but once we walk into that room we are in her domain."

"What idiot asked her to do this seminar anyway?" says Amos.

"This idiot, because she is the best in the region and she is doing it for free," says Shelley. "Don't hate the player, hate the game," says Shelley, giving Adaris a high five.

"Famous last words of two men who are completely and utterly whipped," says Amos.

"Oh, you can talk smack all you want to, you big punk, but a wise man once said, one man's trash is another man's treasure."

"What do you mean by that, Shelley?"

"You'll see in just a few minutes. Oh, and instead of that suit you have on you better go change into your pads. You may need to do some blocking and hitting today. But don't worry about us two utterly whipped men, we got your back!"

# Operation Desert Keeva

"Jackie, I want you to know that this is war. Not bow and arrows, guns and ammo war, but in-your-face chemical warfare war. The kind that involves a sneak attack—and I'm about to take some prisoners."

"The Lord is my shepherd, I shall not want—"

"What the hell are you praying for Jackie?"

"Oh, I'm just praying that we don't have any casualties."

With that the two soldiers of war step into the Tennessee Trailblazers' massive conference room, where they're greeted by Adaris and Shelley.

"Good morning baby," says Adaris.

"Good morning honey, and you too sunshine," says Keeva, walking over to shake hands with Adaris and Shelley.

"Well, I was actually talking to my wife, but it's good to see you as well, Keeva," says Adaris with a grin. "Hmm . . . red. Are you out for power or for blood?"

"Both. You know how it is with you jocks. You don't take anything seriously unless it's football guys or your Mama. I need to show these guys whose boss," says Keeva.

"These boys, or the one huge boy that is over in the corner undressing you with his eyes?" asks Shelley.

"By my account there are several men undressing me. Adaris, you need to stop worrying about me and handle yours. I ain't the only one being undressed," says Keeva.

"Everyone in this room knows I belong to Jackie, make no mistake about it. But just in case they don't know . . ." And with that Adaris runs his hand down Jackie's arm, grabs her hand, and leads her to her seat. He pulls out her chair, waits for her to sit down, and then gently pushes her chair to the table. And then that joker puts Jackie's left hand on the table so everyone can see her mammoth ring and subtly looks around the room making sure everyone is looking. I'm watching every damn move he makes, until I look around at Amos and find him staring at me, not Jackie's ring. I give him a quick eye roll and then look down at my notes to gather myself.

Before I begin any presentation, I always look around the room to get an idea of who my audience is. I note that there are some amazing looking specimens sitting around this conference table, more than 30 men reeking of testosterone. I sense a burning gaze emanating from Amos on my left, and also the curious stare of someone on my right—not the kind that says I am excited about the topic but that I am excited about the presenter. I figure, what the hell. It's nice that someone is paying attention to me, especially since Amos had been so hot and cold over the last few months. My nerves are suddenly calm and my adrenaline kicks in. This is going to be the most interesting hour I've had since the football game when Jackie had to entertain several of Adaris' wanna-be boos.

Shelley gets up to introduce me. I'm actually pretty impressed with myself after hearing his intro. I need to tell Tiffany that Shelley is a keeper.

"Thanks to all of you who are interested in building your individual brand, professionally and personally. As most of you know, pro football players have a reputation for being aggressive, rude, and callous on and off the field. We're the envy of many other athletes because of our strength and prowess, but statistically we have the shortest careers because of the nature of the game. That's also one reason we're the weakest group of athletes financially.

"We created Game Changers to help football players manage their time, talent, and treasure. This marketing session is our first, so let's get going. I'd like to introduce Keeva Hudson-McGhee, the CEO of KeMarketing, a firm Keeva established five years ago to serve small clients. Her main objective is to harness the power and influence we all have inside. Keeva has a B.S. and Master's degree in marketing, from TSU and Vanderbilt. She has designed marketing strategies for 11 Fortune 500 companies and has salvaged the reputations of several businesses, actors, and athletes around the globe. If you need someone to re-create or reshape your image, she is your woman. Today, Keeva is going to give us a broad overview of what she can do to assist us, collectively and individually."

Knowing that I can only hold most people's attention for about 30 minutes, I start by talking about the impact a good image can have on the amount of money an athlete earns over a lifetime. I figure if I get their attention early by talking about money, they're most likely to ask the questions that will let me hit on all my points. I explain that most people in their field typically lose well over two million dollars in their lifetime, and sure enough, they perk up and start asking lots of questions.

I'm getting quite a few questions from a cornerback named Ramsey Knight, the type of questions that lead a sister to think he just might be interested—in me! Most women would consider Ramsey Knight a fine specimen. He's 6 foot 1, has legs that go on forever, and is the color of a nicely browned sugar cookie. But, he is also the perfect example of social media gone wrong, and his reputations is in the cellar. I figure he is the perfect example of why anyone perceived as famous should get professional help to managing their image. For about five minutes the lecture becomes a two-person conversation.

"Ms. McGhee, I have a few questions about the importance of building a positive image, if you don't mind me asking," says Ramsey.

"No, answering questions is why I'm here. Do you prefer Ramsey or Mr. Knight?"

"Most of my friends call me Ram. Can I call you Keeva?"

"I actually prefer Ms. McGhee. Now, what is your question?"

"What can a football player do to enhance their social media image?" Ramsey asks with a cocky smile.

"Mr. Knight, I would suggest that you begin by handling your business on the football field and protecting your personal business off the field."

"What do you mean by that, Ms. McGhee? I have a stellar reputation on the field, I'm a coach's dream, and I'm in the best physical shape of my life," says Ramsey, with another teasing smile.

*This man is trying his best to flirt with me in a room full of people. Now I don't want to go gangsta on his ass, but I think I will have to tell him a little something.* As I ponder the question, out of the corner of my eye I can see Amos glaring at Ramsey from across the table. I decide to let Amos sweat for a few minutes and stay focused on Ramsey.

"Ramsey, I know exactly what your stats are and I am well aware of your physique," I say with a knowing smile. And for good measure I decide to give him a little lookey lookey from the top of his head to his stomach . . . everything else is covered by the table.

"So, Ms. McGhee—and I am assuming that the Ms. indicates you are single?—what else can I do to protect my image? Should I consider settling down soon?"

"Ram, man, I don't think this is the time for Keeva to get into specifics about individual cases. This meeting is meant to offer an overview of what she can do for you. If you want Keeva to be more specific, she and her team can work with you individually," says Adaris.

"Oh, I like the sound of that, Dair. I would love to do a one-on-one with Ms. McGhee, sooner rather than later," says Ramsey as he continues to feast his eyes on me. "But I'd like to have just one tip to help me get started on improving my public image."

This time there are a few chuckles from around the room because it's pretty clear that Ramsey is interested in more than getting 1000 likes on his Facebook page.

"Ms. Hudson-McGhee, let me take this one if you don't mind," Amos says, panning his eyes around the room.

"I really don't need your help, Amos—"

"I am sure you don't need my help, but I think Ram does. Ram, the first thing you need to do to improve your image is to stop procreating with half of Nashville. I know you consider

183

yourself a free agent, but the allegations of you having several baby mamas across the city is bad for your image, and more important, bad for the team and for the game."

"Now wait a minute, Hunt, I was talking to Ms. McGhee," says Ramsey, jumping up from the table.

"Sit your little ass down, man! You asked for it, so you're gonna get it. The next thing you need to do is stop taking inappropriate pictures and showing everyone in the locker room. No one is impressed with your cell phone porn. Should I keep talking, or have you heard enough?"

"Ok, that's enough Amos. You didn't come to this session to attack each other. Ramsey, let's talk about your situation after class. In the meantime, let me give you all a few quick tips you can start on today."

As I'm talking to the players about cleaning up their social media pages and giving back to the community, I can feel the tension emanating from the men on my left and my right. I know Amos has Ramsey by at least 150 pounds, and I'm thankful that the large table is separating the two. I notice that Jackie is wearing a huge smirk. That goat is laughing at me! In truth, I'm actually doing a little laughing on the inside myself. I have never seen Amos get possessive before.

But whether Amos likes it or not, if Ramsey asks for my services on a professional level, I will provide them. I'm not really into the jock type anyway—they are nice on the eyes but sometimes their brains are a little slow on the uptake. Amos is different. He's exceptionally smart and engaging, and not the least bit cocky. He's also confident and modest—I just hope I can talk to him about ways he can improve his image. Hanging out at the strip club might be ok for the younger athletes, but by now he should be beyond pole watching.

My private musings are interrupted when I hear Adaris say, "Ok guys, let's wrap this session up. Shelley and I have a few more items to review with you. Keeva and Jackie will hang around for a few minutes to set up some private consultations. We'll table Jackie's session until next week, since this one ran a little longer than expected," Adaris says, looking at Amos and Ramsey.

Thank God I have a few moments to gather my thoughts before the meeting ends. I didn't mind the little bit of tension, but I'm not sure what will happen next. I certainly don't want the two men to fight over me, even if it was nice to get the extra attention. I did a little cheer inside my head. "I like it I love it, I want more of it."

***

I am in awe as I watch Keeva do her presentation. I knew she had bill-making skills, but this woman is incredible. She really dressed the part in that red dress, and those shoes make her legs look so damn good. I look around the room and see that she has all of these dudes eating out of her hand. I've never been a jealous person, but I am uncomfortable about how Ram is looking at my girl. And what's with asking all those dumb questions? Ram is one of those dudes who has it all. Attended Baylor, got drafted second round his junior year and is pretty enough and is plenty smart, but he thinks he can use his status on the gridiron to get any woman he wants. What Ram doesn't know is that Keeva is not your typical football groupie, and if the dude isn't careful she will have him looking just as pitiful as I feel.

I suddenly sense that Adaris is giving me the look that says, get your shit together! Don't blow everything that we have talked about over the last few months by acting like the big chump you are. Just be cool and let Ram self-destruct.

And then Adaris does something that I will never forget. He pissed on Jackie—a move only those smart enough to notice would catch. What my boy did is lean over and whisper something in Jackie's ear, and her reaction, although subtle, is very telling because the look she gives him is hot enough to burn the toupee off of Coach Pate's head and so damn sexy I almost swoon myself. Then that old retiree looks at me as if to say I need to handle my business with Keeva.

I know he's right. I don't want to blow my chances with Keeva. I need to keep calm and not tackle Ram's little ass. I decide to just stay in my chair and see what happens with

Ram's weak rap. I have a feeling Keeva is going to rip him a new one.

***

As Adaris and Shelley wrap up the meeting, I try to figure out how to avoid both Ramsey and Amos. I'm just not in the mood to deal with Ramsey's weak rap or be ignored by Amos. I start a countdown to see how long it takes him to approach me . . . less than 30 seconds. I must admit, Ramsey has a nice little swagger going as he starts walking my way.

"Ms. McGhee, you not only are good at what you do, you looked damn good up there today. Tell me when we can get together to discuss improving my image—I don't want to lose any more money," Ramsey says with a smirk.

"Here's my card, Ramsey. Give my assistant a call so he can check my schedule."

"Damn your schedule. I want to get together with you as soon as possible. I have a little free time today—we can mix a little business with pleasure, can't we? You down with that?"

"Mr. Knight, I am here in a professional capacity. If you really want me to work with you, then take this card and call my office. Be aware that I will need full disclosure about your past before we can negotiate a contract. Are you willing to do that?"

"Now Keeva, you know I don't kiss and tell. I thought you said today we would focus on the future instead of the past," Ramsey says, moving a little closer to me.

"You don't kiss and tell your mother or your groupie but if you want to work with me, you tell me everything." I glance over at Amos. He hasn't moved an inch. I decide to piss him off a little more and move closer to Ramsey. With my stilettos on I reach his chin. As I step closer, Ramsey's smile gets wider—he looks as if he plans to wrap his arms around me and kiss me.

"Since we're getting more familiar with each other, why don't you answer a few questions for me boo," I say, tilting my head to the side.

"I will answer whatever you want, baby, just as long as we can continue this conversation when we leave here."

I lean closer to Ramsey and turn my body away from Amos so he can't read my lips. I know this red dress makes me look like I have more going on in the rear than usual. "I'm curious about a few things. Is it true that you have three baby mamas and are behind on your child support to two of them? And that two of your children are so close in age they could be considered Irish twins?"

The little punk takes a few steps back. I keep looking directly into his eyes. "And is it true that you stood your fiancé up at the alter a few years ago? And what about the porn you posted on Instagram?"

I finish my little diatribe, and Ramsey crosses his arms over his chest, ever so lightly touching my left breast.

"That is the oldest trick in the book, Mr. Knight."

"What trick are you talking about Ms. McGhee?"

"Crossing your arms so you can cop a feel. Just so you know I don't play those games. If I like you enough you can get a free fill. But if you try that crap again I will have that 6 foot 7 center standing to my right on your ass so fast that you will be six feet under. So, I suggest you back up a few inches. Now I am going to give you some free advice, Mr. Knight. Acting like a bad boy is not cool anymore. One more misstep and the press will crucify you. Most people don't think you should be paid so damn much for playing this ridiculous game, and African American athletes are under the most scrutiny. I suggest you work with someone to clean up your image and to dispel all of this random gossip about you and your jimmy. And speaking of jimmy, you need to learn how to wrap yours up before it falls off. If you are interested in working with me on a professional level to clean up your image, then call my assistant. If not, lose my damn card."

Ramsey looks at me intently for a minute, then says, "I'll call your office tomorrow to schedule a meeting."

"I might change my mind about you, Mr. Knight. You are much smarter than people give you credit for," I say, then I march off in a huff.

"Hey, Ms. McGhee, who is Jimmy?" Ramsey yells as I walk out of the conference room.

As I'm heading for the door, I hear Amos call my name.

"Keeva, Keeva, hold up a minute. I want to talk to you!"

I'm just itching for another fight, and I swing around so fast that Amos jumps back. "Now is not a good time, Amos'."

"What happened in there Keeva?" Amos says, grabbing my elbow.

"It's none of your damn business, Amos. You haven't been concerned about what's happening with me in weeks, so don't pretend to give a damn now!"

"I can tell you're upset and I'm about two seconds from kicking Ram's pretty ass. So I suggest you tell me what is going on or I'll find out for myself."

"Did you not listen to a word I've said for the last hour, you big bully?"

"I would suggest you tone your voice down, Keeva. People are watching."

"I don't give a rat's ass. You men are the ones with image problems, not me!"

"How about we move this conversation into another room so you can tell me what happened."

"Get your hands off of me. I am not going anywhere with you Amos!"

"You have two choices. You can walk your gorgeous self into that room about 20 feet away or you can be carried. Either is fine with me. I can either watch your butt or I can carry your butt so you decide."

I stand there madder than hell, trying to decide if I should call Amos' bluff. But then as my eyes travel from his feet to his face, which is a very long trek, I see in his eyes that he isn't playing with me. I decide to appease him this one time.

"I'll go with you this time, Amos, so you won't be embarrassed in front of your little playmates!"

We walk into another room with massive furniture. I hear the sound of the door locking and quickly swing around to confront Amos.

"What the hell do you want, Amos?"

As I continue my little rant, Amos slowly walks toward me. I can see the look in his eyes, and it is not good. I start backing up until I reach the edge of the table. Amos puts his arms on the table on both sides of me and bends down to my eye level.

"What did you say, Keeva?"

"Well, uh, I said, why are you trying to talk to me now . . ."

"That isn't what you said. But what I want to say is that you did an amazing job today and I am proud of you." As Amos talks, he moves his hands slowly down my arms. I am about to

191

close my eyes and purr like a cat, when it hits me that Amos is trying to seduce me in the Trailblazers stadium!

"What are you doing Amos?"

Amos just smiles and gathers his large hands around my waist. "What do you think I'm doing, Keeva?"

He starts gently kneading my waist and leans down to kiss me softly. He keeps kissing me until I hear myself whimper. "That's it, baby," Amos says, now moving his kisses down my neck. He moves the strap of my dress and gently bites my shoulder.

Before I lose my senses I look at him and whisper, "I want you to stop playing games with me and take us both out of our misery," I say, locking my legs around his huge hips.

"I'm not playing games. When you were bantering with that fool Ram I was jealous as hell, even though I knew you would chew his ass up and spit him out."

By now my straps are down to the middle of my arms and Amos is continuing his journey from my collar bone to the edge of my bra. "So, instead of calling me to say 'I miss you, I want to see you,' you drag me in here like a caveman?"

Amos gently grabs my head and pulls it back so he can look me in the eye. "If I have to drag your little ass into a room and kiss you senseless to get you to beg for more, damn it I'll bite. Now lift that fine ass up off the table so I can get to the good part," Amos says as he slips my dress down over my hips. "Damn, no panties!"

As I'm getting seduced on the Trailblazers conference table I couldn't help thinking how many other women had been in just this position. And then I remember that wives, lovers, and groupies aren't given access to this area of the stadium. Just then someone knocks on the door! And then I realize that Amos and I are about to get our groove on in the middle of the conference room table in broad daylight with a stadium full of players, coaches and staff members with no protection!

Amos lifts his head from my breast and yells, "What!"

"Hey man, it's Shelley. We've been looking for you and Keeva. Is she in there with you? And why is the door locked?"

Amos gives my breast a squeeze, takes a deep breath, and says, "Keeva has come and gone man. I closed myself in here so I could straighten my head out for a few moments." Then he gently places his groin as close to my pocketbook as possible without full penetration.

"Well, her car is still out here and Jackie is looking for her to get a ride home. Should I tell Jackie to leave without her, or do you think maybe you can find her in the next few minutes," Shelley says, laughing.

"Tell Jackie to wait for a few minutes. She just might come at any time now," Amos says as he continues to rub against me.

By that time I am a goner. I can't take it anymore, so I whisper in Amos' ear, "If you don't get rid of him he is going to hear you scream." Then I bite his ear.

"I'll be out in a minute to help you look for Keeva," Amos calls to Shelley.

"All right man, you know how the old saying goes—follow your nose, it always knows!"

As we hear Shelley walk away, Amos eases himself inside me and starts a rhythm that is so sweet I almost swoon.

"Amos, you aren't wearing a condom," I say, nearly breathless.

"I just got tested for everything a few weeks ago," Amos says, continuing his slow grind. "And baby, I never went bareback with anyone before. You're the first," he says, looking deeply in my eyes.

He continues his hypnotic movement, and just before I climb the stairway to heaven, I look at him and say, "If I find out you're lying, you won't have to worry about doing this again because I will cut your di—"

Those are the last few words out of me for several minutes.

As we're getting dressed, I start to feel guilty. This little love fest aside, the issues between Amos and me are still in full effect. Before I can say anything, Amos leans his forehead against mine and says, "We will talk, baby. I promise. Let me wrap a few things up here and I'll come over this evening, ok?"

"Speaking of wrapping up bring your medical records. I think that not only do we need to talk about your little fit of jealousy but we also need to talk about where this is going and how this little romp could impact us." I get down from the table, pull my red power dress down over my hips, and walk out of the conference room with as much dignity as I can. I'm not sure I am looking forward to our little talk this evening . . .

When I reach my car I find two notes under the wiper. The first note says, *"Thanks for the great advice. Call me, Ramsey."* I guess he didn't get the hint. The next note says, *"Call me when you get finished with your meeting with Amos. Toodles, Jackie."*

I figure I better get this phone call with Jackie over with during my drive home, or not only will Jackie be on me like white on rice but so will Serena and Max. Those girls talk too damn much, and I'm not in the mood to be the butt of anyone's jokes once again. But I really needed to call my shrink before I call Jackie. The only man I have ever been intimate with without protection was my ex-husband—what made me do something like that with Amos?

I dial Jackie's number on my hands free as I zoom down the interstate.

"Hello!"

"I got your little note, Jackie. I guess you wanted me to call so you could gloat?"

"I actually wanted you to call so I could make sure you were ok. One minute I see you talking to Ramsey, and the next I see you stomping away with Amos on your heels. And then Adaris says he can't find you!"

*Note to self: when you see Shelley, give him a big hug for not giving me away.*

"Amos and I were having a crucial conversation. He's coming over to my house later so we can start part two."

"Well, I hope you come to some type of agreement on the direction your relationship is going. Take it from me, the cat and mouse game gets really old. By the way, you knocked it out of the park during the meeting, girl. Twelve people signed up to have a consult with you."

"Oh damn . . ."

"Why did you say that, Keeva? This is a great opportunity for you to get some new clients."

"I know it Jackie, but I ain't in the mood to deal with a bunch of inflated egos. Amos is enough!"

"Then use Kyle and other people on your team. No one says you have to do all the work yourself."

"Good point, girl. Ask Adaris to fax the list to my office so we can start setting appointments."

"Will do. Oh, and cousin, the next time I see you, you'll have to tell me what you think of the coaches' meeting room. I'm partial to the locker room myself." And with a peel of laughter Jackie hangs up the phone.

*Damn that Shelley!*

One shower and two hours later, Amos rings the doorbell. I'm not sure how to act, so I open the door with a flourish and wave Amos in.

"No 'hello baby' kiss?"

"You'll get a kiss of life or death once I see your test results."

"I have them right here. But you need to do some sharing as well. You can't see mine if I can't see yours!" says Amos, with a chuckle.

"I think we've seen enough of each other for today. I'm mortified about getting my groove on in the coaches' conference room. You would pick that room!"

"If my memory serves me correctly, you were the one who told me to get rid of Shelley before you made me scream. I'm the one who should feel violated."

"Hmm . . . have a seat on the couch and let me grab my records so we can do a proper exchange. And if you have anything showing as positive I want you to know that I am going to kill you."

I grab my paperwork and hand it to Amos, who is stretched out on my couch as if he owns the place. I look over his medical records and don't see anything I need to worry about.

"Ok, let's see here Amos. Looks like negative for human growth hormones, a little arthritis setting in but overall bone density is good. CT scans of your large brain look good. Negative for HIV, AIDs, Chlamydia, and Herpes. How have you managed to remain unscathed after all of these years?"

"I take care of my body. I told you, you have nothing to worry about. But I see I should be a little concerned about you, Keeva."

I spring up from the chair and say, "What are you talking about?"

"Well, your cholesterol and blood pressure are a little elevated. And your A1C is borderline. Looks like if you don't get this under control soon you may have to start meds. What's up with that, munchkin?"

"Well, it's gotten much better since I started working out. My doctor told me if I can cut down on the stress I will be fine. So, Amos, how do you plan to help me alleviate my damn stress?"

"Come here."

I inch toward Amos feeling just a little leery. He pulls me toward him and sets me on his lap, then he says, "What I plan on doing is to take care of you as much as you will allow me to. I know these last few months have been stressful for both of us. I've been waiting for you to give me a sign that you are ready to see where this thing will take us. Today you showed me how much you care about me. I know you don't share yourself intimately with just anyone. Neither do I."

"What do you mean, waiting for a sign? Hell, the sign you put on my back before the race should have told you something—you must know how much I care about you."

"Well, actually, I don't. You have never really told me how you feel, Keeva. Yeah, you are very attentive while we are in the bed, but are you ready to share our relationship with the world?"

"Amos, every man in my life has screwed over me, starting with the man who was my sperm donor. And you know my ex was a chronic cheater."

"Keeva, I think you're missing something. What about your Uncle Shorty, your brother Bo, your cousin Leo. And me? We all love you and only want what's best for you. Not to mention that Adaris, Chris, and Shelley are crazy about you."

"They don't have a choice. They're all related to me or in love with my friends so they have to love me by default. As for you, how long are you going to love me, Amos? One day will you realize that loving someone older than you is more than you bargained for? What about the groupies who hang outside the stadium? Not to mention the stripper named Passion who would love to climb you."

"Who is Passion?"

"Well it's actually the name I would have chosen if I would have become a stripper. My point is the Passions of the world are just waiting for you."

"Keeva, the Passions of the world will climb anything. That's how they get paid. I know we have a lot to work on, mainly you trusting me and me getting used to you being so damn headstrong and independent. Can't we just take one step at a time and see where things lead? I only ask that you be honest with me. If you aren't comfortable or you decide you want to return to the single life, just tell me."

"I have to tell you, Amos, it's been a long time since I've dated one person at a time. I don't really know what that looks like, so I have to depend on you to lead the way. And I need to warn you that I am still working with my shrink on my issues . . ."

"Thanks for sharing that with me. Believe me, I can handle your issues. All of them. I got big love, girl."

"You got big love all right, but I also need you to have accepting love, Amos. I've been around longer than you and have experienced some bad things. I didn't live a pampered childhood like you did."

"Everyone has their own story . . . which is a great segue to my next request. I'm going back home in a few days and I want you to come with me."

"Ugh! Amos, we just decided to start seeing each other seriously, I don't think I'm ready to take a step that big."

"Sure you are. I've met your family and friends, which gives me a lot of insight about you. Now it's time for you to meet my family so you can learn more about Amos."

"This entire day has been overwhelming. Can you give me a little time to think about this?"

"I'll give you until tomorrow. If you think long you think wrong." With that comment, Amos moves me off his lap, gives me a kiss on the cheek, a pat on the butt, and walks out the door.

I am not sure if I should be relieved or mad, so I give Max a call to get her opinion. I've had enough of Jackie and her little mind games today.

The phone rings several times before Max picks up, sounding a little out of breath.

"I know you aren't exercising and Chris has got to be working out, so you aren't on the love train. Why are you out of breath?"

"What has you in such a chipper mood this afternoon?"

"Well, let's see, Adaris booked me a huge meeting with the Trailblazers to discuss marketing. The star cornerback sexually harassed me in front of the entire team. Amos and I had a tryst in the conference room, and tonight he asked me to go home with him."

"Sounds like you had a great day, girlfriend. Now tell me what the problem really is?"

"Amos wants to take our friendship from a booty call to a relationship. What happened to courting, dating, monogamy, and then—"

"You skipped all of that with Amos. You guys are going backwards. Now what is it Amos wants you to do?"

"He wants me to go home with him to Georgia to meet his family. Hell, I don't really like being around some of my own family, let alone anyone else's. Did you know he lives on a farm with vegetables and livestock?"

"Yeah, that's typically what you find on a farm, Keeva. I don't know why you are acting so bougie. Didn't you grow up in the projects? Nothing can be worse than that!"

"Watch it, Max. I only lived in the projects the first six years of my life."

"They say that most of what we learn is in the first few years. Hey that explains why you act so ghetto but I digress! Expand your mental paradigm a little bit and walk into his world. It's been all about you for the last few months, Keeva."

"I forgive you for that caustic remark. You're right, Max, but I feel like a fish out of water. It's hard to go from just

202

hanging out with him from time to time to this. I was happily single and now he's trying to hem me up!"

"There is nothing wrong with being hemmed up, Keeva."

"What about being knocked up, Max?"

"Yes, that would be me. I finally went to the doctor and he confirmed it. I'm about nine weeks now. Are you satisfied?"

"The question is, how do you and Chris feel about being pregnant?"

"I feel lost, confused, and scared as hell. He doesn't know yet."

"What the hell! Are you trying to wind up on that fake ass show 'I didn't know I was pregnant'? Surely he will realize that you've been keeping this from him. Have you ever talked about having children someday?"

"Keeva, it's complicated. You don't have enough time to hear my story, which is one of the reasons I'm keeping this from Chris. I will tell him soon, so please just keep this to yourself."

"Ok girl, I will, but please take care of you."

"I will, and enjoy your time with Amos and his family. You never know, you may just be surprised."

After talking to Max, I realize my little problem of making a commitment to go with Amos just five hours down the road is nothing in comparison to what she and Chris are dealing with. Apparently Max has some serious issues that date back before we met. Going to Georgia for a few days just means I'm committed to seeing Amos' side of things, right? Who am I kidding? I am about to meet the man's Mama, and his Mama's Mama. As I pick up the phone to call Amos, I get nervous.

"Hello."

"Amos, its Keeva, and I will go."

"You will go where, Keeva?" Amos asks with a chuckle.

"I will go to Macon to meet your family and all the animals and such."

"Are you calling my family animals?"

"No, but I have one condition."

"Condition? I will allow you one, but once you step into my domain I will be in charge. You got it?"

"I got it, but on the way back I want to stop by Phipps Plaza in Buckhead. There's a purse that is calling my name."

# The Elders Speak

Amos and I decide to leave the following Monday, which gives me a few days to clear my schedule. We will be gone for seven days. A whole week to do whatever a city girl from Tennessee does in rural Georgia.

I decide to pay Aunt Ella a visit. Since my mother passed away she has become a surrogate mother to me. Although I talk to my girls about a lot of things, they really don't take me seriously. The problem with acting so tough all the time is you can rarely remove that hat. Aunt Ella lets me wear whatever hat I need to. Jackie mentioned that Aunt Ella is cooking some of her famous perch fish with pork and beans and mashed potatoes, so I decide to invite myself over for dinner.

Aunt Ella recently became a wine connoisseur and joined a local wine club. I figure a nice bottle of Pinot Grigio will help loosen up our conversation. After a plate of food and a few glasses of wine, Aunt Ella gets down to the nitty gritty.

"What's on your mind, baby? As much as I love your company, I know you aren't inclined to come see me in the middle of the week unless you need to talk."

"Aunt Ella, I'm sure you know that Amos and I have been seeing each other on and off for the last few months."

"You know I don't get in you girl's business, but it's pretty easy to see that love is in the air," Aunt Ella says with a smile.

"Love! More like lust. Well maybe I am . . ."

"Lying?"

"Aunt Ella, I really don't know what the heck it is. We started hanging out just to have a little fun, and then he started getting serious on me."

"And then, let me guess—you gave chase."

"Yes, I gave chase and he slow walked me down. Then I started ignoring him and then he started ignoring me—which pissed me off, by the way."

"So now who's chasing whom?"

"I think we both have been caught, or at least we're caught up. I swore after my divorce that I wouldn't get involved with anyone else seriously. It's too much of a hassle. And then this big man comes barreling into the room and . . ."

"And you realized that you actually like him."

"Not just that, but he doesn't take any crap from me Aunt E. I mean, he lets me be myself but I can't run over him like I did the others."

"You mean you can't run him *off* like all the others in the past," says Aunt Ella.

"Yeah, that. There are so many reasons why he isn't right for me." Seeing Aunt Ella raise her eyebrow, I hesitate.

"Let me take a sip of wine before you tell me this one."

"Well, he's younger than me. He plays a brutal and dangerous sport. He is country as hell and he is big. Not to mention that he's a farmer from Macon, Georgia!"

"So your point is?"

"My point is he scares the shit out of me! Sorry Aunt E!"

"It's nothing I haven't heard before, but you do know that you can do worse right? Amos is very mature, extremely gifted, a great football player, and, my goodness, everyone south of the Mason Dixon line is considered country."

"I could do worse?"

"Oh, honey, you know about worse. You were married to him for five years. But he was 'your type,' right? Family from the right side of Chicago. Business major. Great looking and seemingly smart. But, in fact he wasn't worth killing."

"What does that mean, Aunt Ella?"

"What I mean is, he sold you for a bill of goods. He was a wolf in sheep's clothing. The boy was faker than a three dollar bill. Loving you was right, but he was just wrong."

"So why are you telling me all this now Aunt Ella? You could have saved me all those years of heartache if you'd have told me before I married!"

"No one could tell you that, Keeva. Some things you can only find out for yourself. I know that divorce was hard on you. Women in our family either never get married or stay married forever. We don't divorce. And we know what the

Bible says about divorce. God hates it. But the Word also tells us to marry someone who is equally yoked. You two were far from that. So you made a mistake by marrying the one God didn't intend for you. You must forgive yourself and move on. I do believe your and Amos' eggs are aligned."

"But what if they aren't, Aunt Ella? What if taking this step to meet his family is a mistake?"

"You will never know if you don't take the step, Keeva. I've always marveled at how fearless you can be when it comes to business but so skittish about affairs of the heart. Going to Macon is not jumping the broom, honey."

"Ok, Aunt Ella. This chicken is going to Georgia, but I sure as hell hope that I don't come home to roost. Speaking of yokes, Aunt E, what is going on with Mr. Fulton?"

"Skip and I are just friends, Keeva. We've known each other for a long time and have a lot in common. So don't go jumping to conclusions."

"Oh, I see the looks Mr. Fulton gives you. And I see you have been having some late night coffee breaks."

"Niece, I am just as easy on the eyes as all of my girls. Why wouldn't he be looking?" Ella says with a bright smile.

"Aunt Ella, I am so glad to see that smile on your face once again. I can't tell you how much I have missed it."

"I had a wonderful marriage. I know where your uncle is and my children are doing well. What is there not to smile about," Aunt Ella replies, leaning over to give me a hug. "Now get out of here. You have some packing to do."

***

At the same time as the wine and fish fry another meeting was taking place among Amos and Aunt D via the telephone.

"Aunt D, its Amos. Do you have time to talk for a few minutes?"

"Darling, at the age of 87 I have nothing but time. How is your chess game going, dear?"

"We're in the middle of the game and I'm hoping that Keeva is about ready to resign."

"Tell me more, big boy! I haven't been this excited since the summer of 1977!"

"I want to hear more about that someday, Aunt D," Amos says, laughing. "I have collected a few pawns and I almost have her bishop."

"Just tell me what's going on in layman's terms."

"Keeva is going to Macon with me next week to meet my family."

"Well, I would say that is progress, but make sure you stay a step ahead of Keeva. My niece is very smart, but she is also a runner. Make sure she stays in the game."

"What do you mean, Aunt D?"

"You're taking her completely out of her environment, which I am sure has her very nervous. You need to continue to strip away all things from her world and submerge her as deeply as you can in your own. She needs to know that she can operate in both places."

"Got it, Aunt D. I'll give you a call when we return. Thanks again for the wonderful advice."

"You are very welcome, my child. Now go get your queen!"

## Georgia on My Mind

Early Monday morning, Amos picks me up in a vehicle so loud that I actually hear him before I see him. The truth is, I hear a car barreling down the street and I curse the teenager who must surely be driving the contraption . . . then I realize that said contraption is idling outside my house. I peek out the window and see the biggest truck I've ever laid eyes on. This man never ceases to amaze me. First a Hummer and now a Ford F350. You can take the boy out of the country but, oh well. I prepare myself to answer the door, and when I open it, Amos' mouth drops open.

"Keeva baby, we're going for five days, not two months. What on earth possessed you to pack five suitcases?"

"The same thing that possessed you to pick me up in that big ass truck. It's certainly big enough for my little bit of luggage. I haven't been to a farm since the third grade so I had no idea what to pack."

"I told you—jeans, shorts, t-shirts, a couple of hats, and a few pairs of boots, babe," Amos said, leaning over to brush my lips with a kiss.

I lick my lips and reply, "I didn't know if I should bring my riding, cowboy, rain, or designer boots, so I brought all of them."

"How many, Keeva?"

"How many what?"

Amos crosses his arms and raises his eyebrows.

I walk over to Amos, pull his head down to give him, another kiss and say, "I lost count at 15."

"You better be glad you got sweet kisses or I'd make you unpack about half of those shoes."

"I didn't know if I needed the Uggs, Bear Claws, Fryes, or Ralph Laurens . . ."

Amos leans down to lick my lips and give me a hint of tongue, and then he says, "I don't know who most of those people are, but I know those daisy dukes are only appropriate for our five-hour ride. I told you to wear something comfortable. It looks like you didn't have enough room for some regular size shorts. But I ain't mad at ya."

"Let go of my butt, Amos. I knew wearing these shorts was not the best idea. And I can't dress like comfort to meet your family."

"You have all your teeth, most of your hair, and you meet the height requirements—to be a great jockey—you will do just fine," Amos says, giving me another hard squeeze on the behind.

As we walk to the car I ask, "What's with the F350 Amos? The Hummer isn't big enough?"

"Not for your luggage, my supplies, and all the shopping you'll force me to do on our way home. Hop in so we can get through Atlanta before the afternoon traffic hits."

"You never told me what you have planned for the week, Amos."

"A little of this and a little of that. My main goal is to introduce you to the wonders of living off the land and to real organic food right at the source—not in the stores where it carries inflated price tags."

"Since I don't spend much time in the grocery store, it's all new to me."

"Well little bit, you'll be in Hunter's Haven for the next few days." And with that he leans over to fasten my seat belt, pulls out of the driveway in the surprisingly smooth truck, and turns up the music. As I listen to the music and the surprisingly calm beat of my heart, I look over and study Amos through my sunglasses. For the first time in a long time I really look at him. His unique features create a striking canvas. His skin is a Hershey bar chocolate color, and his large forehead reflects the strength of our forefathers. Amos has large eyes that sparkle, a long narrow nose, wide lips, and beautiful teeth. He also has a football player's huge neck, larger than life shoulders, and a massive chest that curves down to his flat stomach. As my eyes lazily move down his body I skip over the lower region. I can't afford to go there right now, so my eyes just roam over his gigantic thighs and calves.

"Do you like what you see?" Amos drawls with a light chuckle.

"How did you know I was checking you out?"

"Well, the angle of your body is a dead giveaway, not to mention the little hum I keep hearing from your mouth."

"I was just thinking about how well you are put together for someone so . . ."

"So big. Well, big doesn't necessarily mean obese. I take great care of my body. I exercise every day in season and out, and I try to eat like people did in the Old Testament. That's why it's so important for me to encourage people to live off of their own land."

"I admire your discipline, and I want to hear more about your ideas about healthy eating. I thought my genes would protect me, but after Rena and I did a study of our genealogy on our maternal side of the family, I realized that I could be in trouble. It helps that I started exercising, but I need to know and do more. Aunt D may have reached 87 in amazing shape, but most adults in our family don't live over age 60."

"Well, the timing for our little getaway is perfect. We can focus all week on clean living. We have about four more hours to go, so I suggest you get some rest, darling, and stop ogling me."

"I didn't wear these shorts for nothing, Amos."

"Oh, believe you me, while you're resting I'll be sneaking some peeks at those fantastic legs. But once we get to Hunter's Haven I need you to put on some longer pants. If not, I and about 50 other people won't get anything done this week."

As I close my eyes and start to relax, it hits me that for the first time in a very long while I am considering someone else's opinion about what I wear. In fact, the only person I considered when putting on my shorts was Amos. So what's bothering me about that flippant comment he made? I realize it's not the comment but the fact that I was positioning myself to consider someone else's opinion and feelings. All of a sudden my well-shod feet get very cold, and as we travel down the road to Macon, I wonder if I'm actually going down the proverbial rabbit hole.

### Harlem, New York

I wake up suddenly, feeling like my stomach is about to turn over. My first instinct is to jump up out of bed, but Chris' arms are locked around me and he's quietly snoring into my neck. Oh God, please help me peel his arms away and get to the bathroom before I throw up in the bed. I move as gingerly and quickly as I can, swallow the bile in my throat, and sprint to the bathroom on the far side of Chris' brownstone so he won't be able to hear me.

I empty my stomach and then sit on the toilet seat with my head resting in my hands. Maxine Isadora Hilton, what the hell have you gotten yourself into? You meet the most popular person in the state of New York, let him take what is left of your virginity, and then you get pregnant—by a man who is adamant about not wanting kids! And who am I kidding? After my jacked up childhood I don't want kids either. Yet here I am, nine weeks pregnant and thousands of miles from home with nowhere to run.

Max Hilton, attorney extraordinaire, tough as nails professor, the one who supposedly has her shit together is sitting on a cold toilet seat in her boyfriend's house scared to death to talk to him. Thankfully nobody can tell I'm pregnant yet, and Chris is getting up so early to go train and work out that he has missed my bouts of morning sickness.

As I sit in the bathroom, I realize it's time. I can no longer hide my secret from Chris. It's bad enough that Keeva knows. Even though my secret is safe with her, it isn't fair to hide something this important from my child's father.

Feeling resigned and resolved, I get up, rinse my mouth out, wipe the sleep out of my eyes, and put on my best trial face. I open the door to find Christopher Map standing right in front of the door with his arms spread from one side of the jamb to the other.

"What the hell is going on, Max?"

"Good morning Chris."

"Good morning Max. Now are you going to answer my question?"

As he bores into me with those honey brown eyes, I take a deep breath. My eyes can't help but travel from his frowning mouth to his beautifully toned arms, then down to his naked pecs and torso. But before I can finish my visual journey, I hear the voice that helped make him the longtime captain of his team.

"Max, answer my question!"

"I suggest you check your tone. I am not one of the mindless groupies you can intimidate. Now move out of my way so I can get out of the bathroom!"

"I am not moving an inch until you tell me why you have had no period in the last two months, why your stomach has been hurting, why you have lost weight, and why you are throwing up in the bathroom on the other side of the apartment, even though you skipped dinner last night. Are you anorexic Max?"

*Is this Negro kidding me! Hell, I wish I was anorexic! A shrink and a balanced diet could get rid of that problem, but my current situation is going to last a lifetime!*

217

"Anorexic?"

"Yes. Anorexic! I'm really concerned about you."

"Well I . . ."

Chris suddenly grabs me, yanks me into his arms, and says, "I think we need to schedule an appointment with my doctor today and get you checked out baby. I want you to start feeling better."

As I stand there with my body plastered against his chest, I realize that Chris doesn't have a clue. But why not? He just described all the signs of pregnancy—I guess that is just the last thing on his mind.

I pull back and look into his eyes, where I see concern, love and adoration. I feel a chill run through my body, one so profoundly cold that I start shivering. Somehow I know beyond a shadow of a doubt that my confession will forever alter our fragile relationship. But I also know that, no matter what, Chris deserves to know he is going to be a father.

I grab his head and caress his face and say, "Baby, I'm fine."


"You are not fine Max. You haven't been yourself in weeks, and you look sad. Tell me!"

"Well, I'm not fine, but I will be in about thirty one weeks."

"So you did go to the doctor. What did he say?"

"Well, she said we'll be having a baby in a few months."

I'm not sure how long we stand there in front of that bathroom door. I see every emotion pass across Chris' face, from surprise to shock to confusion, and, lastly, anger. Everything except happiness and joy.

"Did you hear me baby? I said we're expecting a child, Chris."

And then his arms fall away from my body and the chill returns. Those beautiful honey brown eyes have become cold and detached. I step back so far that I fall onto the toilet seat. Chris moves forward and stoops down in front of me.

This time he grabs my face with one hand, narrows his eyes and says, "I know I didn't hear what you said. I need you to repeat it."

"I am pregnant!"

"By whom?" Chris asks, tightening his hand around my face.

I swat his hand away and say, "What in the hell do you mean, by whom? Who in the hell have I been with for the last year?"

"Shit, you obviously need to ask yourself that question, Max!"

"You son of a bitch! I gave my virginity to you because I love you, and you have the audacity to ask me who the father of my child is!"

Chris jumps up and starts pacing. I sit on the toilet seat and watch him, fear and confusion gripping my heart. He finally stops and says, "Who is the father of the child, Max?"

"It's you, you asshole! Why in the hell would I lie to you about this?"

"Because I am sterile, Max! I have known for the last two years that I can't have children!"

"What! Who told you that foolishness? Because they are obviously wrong, Chris! And why in the hell didn't you tell me?"

"Two doctors told me. When my ex-wife and I were contemplating divorce, I found out she had been taking birth control pills. Then we decided to try to salvage our marriage. For some stupid reason we thought having a child might save us. We tried for almost a year, and when we couldn't get pregnant we went to a fertility doctor. We both had a battery of tests and I found out that I'm sterile, due to a severe case of the mumps when I was little. I went to a specialist who confirmed it. So there is no way in hell you can be pregnant by me. And the funny thing is, during most of our marriage my wife tried not to get pregnant, and then when we actually wanted to it was me who kept it from happening!"

"But the doctor is wrong, Chris! I haven't been with anyone other than you . . . ever."

Chris swings around and starts laughing. "It's damn near impossible to reverse sterility, Max. You want to know why I didn't tell you? I didn't tell you because I wanted to make sure you weren't some gold digging groupie who just wanted me for my money, like my ex-wife and all the others. I wanted to see if you really cared about me as a person before I shared something that intimate about me. You see, I thought you were different Max. I was shocked when I found out you were a virgin, but now I realize maybe that shit wasn't true. I guess I was so excited that you'd share something so precious with me that I trusted you. But as soon as I decide to really share my life with you, you tell me you're pregnant by someone who obviously isn't me. I thought I had seen it all with my ex, but you take the cake. Now get your shit and get out of my house and my life. Go to the man that you screwed behind my back and tell him he is about to be a father, because the damn jig is up. You won't get one red cent from me!"

Chris storms out of the room and slams the door. I feel more alone than I have since I was an eight-year-old girl. I know I can't call Jackie or Keeva. I'm too embarrassed and humiliated. I have to take what's left of my broken heart and pride and get the hell out of here.

Luckily I've kept my clothes in a guest bedroom so I don't have to face Chris. My experience today is mirroring what happened 22 years ago. As I walk to the bedroom wiping tears

221

from my eyes, I resolve once again that I will never let another man screw me and then send me away.

I wipe away my tears, get dressed, and pack my bags. I won't beg Chris to hear me out or try to change his mind. I have too much pride for that. I'll fly home to St. Croix today, take care of myself and my unborn child, and once it is born I'll make Christopher Warren Map pay in ways he could never imagine. By the time I finish proving that he's the father of our child, humiliate him in the press, and take a good chunk of his money, he'll wish he had never called me a liar. And he can forget ever laying an eye our child!

# The Evolution

"Amos, I can't do this!"

"Yes you can Keeva. Just push a little harder."

"But you said you wouldn't make me squeeze if I rode in front."

"Well I lied. You really need to squeeze Keeva. Come on, it will make me feel good."

"Ok, Amos, but this is it. You know I like getting dirty, but this takes dirt to another level."

"That's it baby! Right there. Now keep that groove."

"Oh my gosh, the milk is actually coming out Amos. I am actually milking a cow!"

"I told you, you would get the hang of it if you would just try it Keeva. Now keep that movement and you will have almost a gallon of milk in a few minutes.

"Who ever thought milking a cow would be this exciting. Just to think that today I rode on the front of a horse without your help, fed the chickens and now I am milking a cow."

"And to make it even better I have it all on tape so if you start tripping in the future I will just pull out my cell phone and show this little recording," says Amos with a Cheshire grin.

"You wouldn't Amos!"

"No I... well I might Keeva. These last few days have been great. Once you finally loosened up and relaxed you really started to get a feel for what farming is all about.

***

We're finally back, seven long days after we left. We spent six days on Amos' family farm in Macon, and then one day at the malls of Lenox and Phipps to make up for the first six days. I came back three shades darker, with several bruises, a nappy head—and a new fall wardrobe! I won't say the visit was actually hellish, but there were some moments I did feel like I was in another world.

I need the entire day to get my hair done, get a mani/pedi, and get my five broken fingernails repaired. There is no way I can go back to work tomorrow looking like who shot John! About an hour after Amos drops me off in his mammoth truck, I send a text out to my girls to set up a conference call for 7:00 this evening. At 6:57 I dial the line and wait for everyone to join. Of course Serena is already on the phone because she is never late for anything, and Jackie is a close third.

"Good evening ladies of the night. What's good?"

"The only person who sees this lady at night is Micah," says Serena with a snort.

"Hey cousin. I can't wait to hear about your trip, especially since we didn't hear a mumbling word from you the whole time you were gone. And I don't think we need to wait on

Max. I've been trying to call her for the last two days and she hasn't called or texted me back."

"I thought you might say that Jackie. Has Adaris talked to Chris this week? I was wondering if Max was still up north hanging out with him."

"Yeah, he talked to Chris, but just briefly, since camp is about to start. And he didn't ask if Max is still there, so I'm not sure where she is."

"Hmm . . . well, she'll pop up when it's time. You know how Max is," says Rena.

"She'll pop up alright . . ."

"What did you say?" Jackie asks.

"Nothing girl. So, is anyone going to ask me about my trip?"

"Isn't that the reason we're on this call Keeva? Tell us what happened on the farm."

"Well, in the first place, the farm is more like a ranch, a successful multi-million-dollar ranch at that."

"What you talking 'bout Willis? I thought Amos was a small town country boy."

"I thought the same thing, but we thought way wrong on this one. He's a third-generation farm boy whose third generation took a semi-successful pecan farm and made it into a smooth operating machine. Any of you heard of Hunts Nuts?"

"Who hasn't heard of Hunt's Nuts? I buy them all the time, they're the best pecans in the South."

"Well, my darling, those pecans are grown and packaged by Amos' family. Not to mention that the company has a branch that helps impoverished neighborhoods across the country establish community gardens."

"Wow girl! And you thought Amos Hunter was a big goofy center from Macon, Georgia, who spent his time at the strip club. Who knew that you would meet the king of nuts!" says Jackie.

"I still think he's a goofy center, but now I know he's also a highly intelligent and independently wealthy man and his nuts are definitely the best. But, we were still on a farm all week, and his family is literally well . . . nuts. At least some of his extended family.

"So is his mom as big as her pictures?" Rena asks.

"The whole damn family is big, but Amos' mom is absolutely beautiful in all her bigness, and she is also the CEO of the company. I thought I might be able to give her some advice, but she took me to school. She also kept calling me a little wisp of a thing and asked me several times how I plan to push out her grandchildren, since Amos weighed 11 pounds when he was born."

"Damn girl, can you say C-section! Don't even try getting a big ass Amos Jr. out the traditional way," Jackie says with a laugh.

"There is enough baby-making going on to last me for a while girl. Babies are not on my mind at this point."

"So what about the rest of the family? And what the heck did you do for an entire week?" asks Rena.

"Well, he has two older brothers, both in the military. One is still active and one recently retired and is working for the company. He has three sisters, one of whom is also in the military. One works for the company, and the other is at Harvard Business School finishing up her MBA so she can come back and work for the company. The Hunter ranch is 500 acres. Each child gets ten acres of land to build a home on when they turn 25. Twenty acres belong to Amos' parents, and the rest belongs to the extended family. Those are the acres they use for farming, and they can't be divided per their great-grandfather's will.

"The first day was overwhelming. Everyone is big and country as hell, but I swear they can cook just as well as the two of you. I gained five pounds while I was there. Amos' brothers are nice, but his sisters are very protective of Amos, since he's the baby boy. I swear they pulled my credit report before I got there, and they asked me every question under the sun. And Amos' Aunt Myra followed me around the entire first day."

"Myra, huh?! While she was following you around was she saying anything?" asks Rena.

"Oh, she said plenty. She told me all about the family. I don't know what she made up and what was true, but by the end of the day I had enough dirt on everyone to last me two lifetimes."

"Well, did you ask Amos?" says Jackie.

"Hell no! One day I'm going to need all that gossip. Myra's secrets are safe with me, at least for the time being."

"So what did you do the rest of the week?" Jackie asks.

"I learned how to ride a horse, which was pretty amazing, especially when Amos was teaching me. He rode with me the first few times until I got the hang of it. And don't go there Rena. I know you're thinking of saying something nasty, and believe me, what they say about doing it on a horse is all true."

"You nasty thing. Now tell us about the nuts, girl!" says Serena.

"I'm nasty! Look who's talking. Well, Amos walked me through the process of harvesting pecans. They have thousands of pecan trees that they have to maintain to get a good crop. Once they've picked the pecans, they take them over to the plant where they separate the good from the bad, shell them, and package them for sale. Now I know why pecans are so damn expensive—it takes a ton of pecans to fill up a bag.

Jackie says, "All I want to know is, can you hook a sister up with some pecans? 'Cause they cost a grip in the store."

"I knew you'd ask so I bought 50 pounds of shelled pecans for you. Merry Christmas, girl—even with the discount those nuts cost the same as a pair of really good shoes."

"Well, my budget thanks you. I've been baking a batch of cookies for Adaris and AJ every week, but 50 pounds will hold me for a while. And now that I know that Amos' family is behind Hunt's Nuts I won't buy anything else."

"Well, what did you bring me, little cousin?" Serena says with a laugh.

"Glad you asked that, big cuz. I brought you the best gift of all. Next month you and I will pitch a new marketing plan to Mama Hunter at their headquarters in Macon. The company is doing well, but their advertising and marketing are a little dated. I made some suggestions while I was there and the family seemed to like them . . . well, everyone except Amos' older sister Angel. An angel she is not, but I understand her need to protect her family's fortune—and her brother."

"Thanks cuz. Let's get together later this week and discuss our game plan. Now . . . what happened with Amos? Are you in love or are you still on hold?" Serena asks.

"I love his dirty drawers, and I say that in a literal sense you guys. He not only taught me how to ride and about his family nuts, he also showed me how to milk cows and explained a lot of farming techniques. I swear, that is the hardest and most noble work a person can do, and you can't worry about looking cute or smelling pretty when you do it. You just stick your ass in the air and get down to business," says Keeva.

"I'm a little confused, girl—are you talking about farming or sex?" says Jackie.

"I'm talking about farming, but I swear, watching him handle those big tools is sexy as all get out. And seeing someone grow and nurture the things you put in your mouth is amazing. And then to sit down and eat it fresh on the farm . . . it was orgasmic!"

"So are you going to quit your day job and take up farming Keeva?" laughs Serena.

"No, but I do have to say, all my preconceived notions that farmers are country ass backwards people have been thrown out the window. I have a newfound respect for that occupation."

"So now what Keeva? Wasn't this trip meant for you and Amos to decide the next steps in your relationship?" says Rena.

"It was actually a trip to get Keeva's health under control. How are your blood pressure and cholesterol these days Keeva?" Jackie says with a chuckle.

"I was totally relaxed until I got on this call with you two morons—I can already feel my pressure going back up. I knew I should have called Aunt Ella instead of you two."

"You still didn't answer the question Keeva. Are you in or out? And hurry up, because I need to go!" says Rena.

"That's a great question, smart ass. One that I don't really have an answer to. If anything, this trip confused me even more. In a way, I'm not sure if I'm good enough for Amos. He comes from good stock, has a shitload of money, and he loves his Mama. But I also know he really cares about me,"

"Are we talking about livestock or a man, 'cause you lost me at the 'good stock' part," says Jackie with a yawn.

"I'm so happy that this conversation is putting you to sleep Jackie. You know good and got damn well I am talking about Amos. And to answer your question, the jury is still out. Now I'm going to hang up the phone so the two of you can roast me. Goodbye!"

After Keeva hangs up, the two sisters burst out laughing and they agree that more bridesmaid dresses will be needed very soon. Before they get off the phone, they say a prayer for their dear friend Max. No one mentioned it, but they all sense that their friend is in turmoil.

231

***

"What's up Dair, did you miss me?"

"Actually, this last week has been the most peaceful for Jackie and me in a long time. We didn't have to spend half our day talking to you and Keeva. So no, I did not miss you."

"Well, Amos is sorry to hear that, especially since he brought you some vegetables from the farm and my mom sent you some homemade jam, not to mention the pecans Keeva brought for Jackie."

"Ok, man, I did miss you! So much that Jackie and I will be inviting you over to dinner this week—we can cook up some of the loot you brought," says Adaris.

"That sounds more like it. Hey man, what's up with World? I tried to holler at him a few times while I was in Macon and his phone kept going to voicemail. Max doesn't have him hemmed up like that, does she?"

"I don't know what's going on with Chris, man. I talked to him for about two minutes last week, but he was real short and didn't sound like his usual self. Jackie has been trying to get in touch with Max and she isn't calling back. I know how World is—he'll call when he feels like talking."

"Yeah, I guess so man. It's not like him not to answer my calls, but you know him better than I do, so I will trust your judgment."

"So, how was the trip?"

"It was straight."

"Ole girl meet the folks?"

"Met them and made a connection."

"Is she still a keeper?"

"Still slow walking her down."

"How did she deal with all the cheese your folks have?"

"Shocked for a minute, but she recovered."

"Can she handle the future?"

"Well . . . I didn't tell her about all of that yet."

"You forgot to tell her, or you are going to wait to tell her?"

"Going to wait."

"Cool, then keep doing what you're doing."

"Bet. Will keep you posted."

"Don't wait too long. You know she's like a bloodhound."

"More like a piranha, but I get your drift."

"You tell her how bad you were feeling her?"

"Yeah man, I did."

"How did that go?"

"Not sure . . . things were hot and heavy when I said it. Jackie close by?"

"Yep."

"Hmm . . . see you tomorrow at the gym?"

"Yeah dude. Holler."

As Jackie walks past Adaris, she asks, Honey, was that Chris on the phone?"

"No babe, just doing a little follow-up work with Amos."

# Don't Ask, Don't Tell

Jackie and I haven't seen each other in over a week, so we decide to meet for lunch. I've been out of the office for so long it's hard to focus, so I figure a long lunch won't hurt. We decide to meet at a restaurant downtown. I arrive before Jackie, so I grab us a booth and order a glass of wine.

"You must really be relaxed to be having a drink in the middle of the day. What the heck did Amos do to you girl?"

"Give me a hug, cuz. I missed you while I was gone."

Before leaning down to hug me Jackie, puts her hand on my forehead.

"What are you doing?"

"Checking to make sure you didn't fall off the horse and bump your skull."

"Fresh air, good food, and great loving will do it to you. It was a different beat, but the time I spent with Amos was scary good."

Jackie raises a perfectly arched eyebrow.

"What I mean is, my blood pressure is down, my energy is high, and I feel wonderful!"

"So, did you come to any resolution during your field trip?"

"Well, I came to an evolution. I made up my mind that I am going to quit my job, give away all my clothes and shoes, let my hair go natural, and become a housewife."

Before I can take a breath, Jackie spits the water she's drinking across the table and all over the new blouse Amos bought me during our shopping trip.

"Dammit Jackie, if I weren't so relaxed I would kick your butt for messing up my new blouse."

"But since you're giving it away, it's ok, right?" says Jackie with a smirk.

"Lies you tell. I realized last week that I can have the best of both worlds. Amos is a chameleon and so is his family. They have turned a small town farm into a million dollar business. I'm really intrigued by their versatility. They are farmers, career military men, women, athletes, and astute business people. Amos told me that his grandparents made a deal with all their grandchildren that they could pursue any occupation they want, but before they could work for Hunt Industries they had to obtain a bachelor's degree. And each of them who earns a degree has to pay for someone in the next generation to go to school."

"Now that is some kind of inheritance!"

"Yeah girl. There is no way our crazy family could do that."

"So really, Keeva, where did this trip leave you and Amos?"

"Well, he apparently hasn't brought any woman home ever, so I was definitely a topic of conversation and speculation. And I got to see Amos in his element. Since his dad passed away five years ago he's really stepped up. He goes home for a few months every year to work in the company and on the farm. He's been instrumental in educating leaders in major cities about community farming. And I know he loves me Jackie. He doesn't just tell me, he shows me. I'm not petrified anymore, I'm just scared, and for me that is growth."

"So how do you merge your three worlds, Keeva? He apparently plans to go back to Macon when he retires. Could you give up the big city for a small town and a family-run company?"

"I don't know Jackie. The last time I gave up I lost."

"No one said you had to give up anything. And you do know that sometimes you have to lose to gain."

"Yes, but a week away is one thing. I'm not sure I can handle six or seven months a year. What if I don't like it?"

"But you love Amos, right?"

"Whoa . . . I didn't say that."

"But you didn't deny it either, Keeva. Just take one day at a time, girl . . ." Jackie says, as she frowns while watching someone across the room.

"What are you frowning about, Jackie?"

"I don't want you to turn around yet, but you need to see something. Let me just say that I really want you to remember that your pressure is down and that you had a great time last week, ok?"

"Forget that shit, girl." I whip around to see Amos and Jazzmine walking to a booth across the restaurant.

As I sit there watching Amos and Jazzmine begin what looks like a deep conversation, several thoughts run through my mind. The first is, why is it that every time I think I have found the right man some bitch shows up with him in a restaurant? The second thing is, what shoes do I have on today, because my blouse is already ruined and I need to consider whether it's worth messing up my Pradas to kick Amos' ass. But since Amos also bought me these shoes after I messed up my Frye and Ralph Lauren boots, I figure I don't have anything to lose. Jackie squeezes my hand and says, "Keeva, before you turn this mother out, please remember that everybody has a cell phone and can upload videos instantly, and that you just finished a workshop on protecting your public image."

"Oh, I won't do anything to make anyone look bad, Jackie. In fact, I'm going to surprise everyone, especially Amos, and do just the opposite of what he might expect. Now, you hold my earrings and these two rings, just in case a sister needs to change her mind if she doesn't get the right damn answers. And be prepared to call 911."

"But you just said . . ."

Before Jackie can convince me not to walk across the room, I take off. By the time I reach his table, Amos is holding Jazzmine's hand like he is consoling her. I pray that he is breaking up with her. As I get closer, Jazzmine looks up, sees me, and her tears instantly dry up as if she has seen a ghost.

"Hi Jazzmine, and oh, hi Amos. I didn't see you sitting here," I say with a fake smile.

"Hey baby. What are you doing here?" Amos says with a smile as he gets up to give me a hug.

"Stay seated, Amos. And if you don't mind, I think I might sit down myself. Why don't you scoot over Jazzmine so I can cop a squat? Now that the gang is all here, why don't the two of you tell me what is really going on. You two have been having these little hookups since Jackie and Adaris' wedding."

"Keeva, baby, part of having a relationship is building trust. I want you to let me finish my lunch with Jazzmine, and then we can talk, ok?"

"I was trusting you, but you didn't tell me you were meeting Jazzmine, and next thing I know I see you over here holding her hand. So at this point I trust you about as far as I can throw your ass across this room." And then I turn to Jazzmine, who is looking like a deer in headlights, and I say, "Right now my pressure is lower than normal, but it's rising fast, so before I explode, do you want to tell me why I see you pushing up on my man every time I turn around?"

"Your man?" says Amos with a frown.

"You heard me, Amos. Now, will you answer my question please before I go ham up in this piece?"

"Jazzmine, you don't have to answer Keeva if you don't want to."

I swing around to look at Amos, and then I look back at Jazzmine with narrowed eyes.

"Amos, I think it's time we tell Keeva. She needs to know because this will affect her."

"Tell me what? That you two are in a relationship and that you are pregnant, because I swear if that comes out of your mouth I am going to lose my damn mind!"

"Keeva, watch your mouth! Can you give Jazzmine and me a chance to talk? I promise if she is ok with it, I'll tell you what's going on."

"Amos, it's ok. I know this looks pretty bad, Keeva, but it's not what you think."

"Famous last words, Jazzmine. The last time I heard that I was at the doctor getting checked out. Now if you don't—"

"Enough Keeva! Jazzmine, you don't have to say a word. Keeva and I need to be able to set boundaries and—"

Boundaries! I am suddenly leaning across the table to do God knows what when I feel Jazzmine grab my arm.

"No Amos. This has gone on long enough." Jazzmine takes a deep breath, then starts to speak. "Keeva, Amos is really my cousin, at least I think he is. When I started tailoring his clothes over a year ago we started talking, and I found out he is from Macon. I was adopted as a baby, but I've been doing some research for the last few years and found out that my birth mother is also from Macon. My research led me to a woman named Myra Hunter, who is Amos' aunt."

Now Amos speaks up. "And I know for sure that Myra got pregnant when she was 17, and because she is mentally unstable my grandmother decided not to keep the baby in the family. She thought it would be easier for my aunt not to see her child every day, so they gave her to a couple in Kentucky who couldn't have children. My grandmother is deceased, so it's been hard to put the pieces together. My mom tells me they never saw the baby. She was given to the adoption counselor immediately after she was born. All we know is it was a healthy baby girl. When I first met Jazzmine I really felt like I knew her. I've seen some pictures of Myra as a teenager, and she looks a lot like Jazzmine."

"So you're telling me that you two are kissing cousins? Now that is just nasty, Amos. I know a lot of country people practice incest, but that is just too much."

"Even if we weren't cousins there would be none of that Keeva. I'm not in the least bit interested in Amos."

"Now hold your horses, Jazz. My man is fine."

"I agree, but I'm not interested in men, Keeva. I'm actually dating a woman named Chloe Mains."

"Chloe, Chloe. Where have I heard that name before?"

"She's a stylist—she's actually styled your cousin Jackie and your friend Max. But that's another story, girl."

I move a few inches away to get a better look at Jazzmine. "So, you are telling me that all this time the two of you have been trying to figure out whether you're cousins? And you're not interested in Amos?"

"We are 90 percent sure that we are related, but we're trying to figure out when and how to tell Amos' family."

"And Keeva, no one knows about this other than the three of us. I really want to protect Jazzmine's privacy, just in case she decides she doesn't want to pursue meeting her birth mother."

I shake my head and think, Amos' family just one-upped mine. The crazy aunt had an illegitimate child over 20 years ago. Jazzmine is related to Amos, and she likes women. Now that's a story for you. But what I say is, "But the two of you have been making me think there is something going on with you this whole time. Were you trying to make me jealous?"

"Yes!"

"No! Well, I can't speak for Amos, but I was not trying to make you jealous . . . maybe I wanted to make Chloe jealous at one point, but I realized that doing that only causes problems in a relationship—and so should you, Amos. Now, I need to head back to work. Thanks for letting me vent for a few minutes, Amos. And Keeva, thanks for not kicking my ass.

I thought I saw you give your jewelry over to Jackie," Jazzmine says as she scoots out of the booth and gives Jackie a quick wave across the room.

"Feel better now Keeva?"

"What do you mean, Amos?" I say with a sniff.

"You came in, disrupted my lunch, and jumped to conclusions. How many times do I need to tell you that I am not him, Keeva?"

"But Amos, you should have told me—"

"Told you what? You don't always tell me who you're meeting with. But I trust you, even though your reputation is worse than mine when it comes to relationships!"

"What are you saying, Amos?"

"What I am saying, Keeva, is that until you learn how to let go of the past, we can't build a future. Now, while you go back to your table and put your jewelry back on, give that some thought."

And then he walks out of the restaurant.

I take my walk of shame back to the table I never should have left. I am sick and tired of getting too much information and keeping everyone's damn secrets. Not to mention that Amos has just laid me low—a term I learned in country ass Macon from his Mama, which means he broke my face, told me off, and put me in my place all at the same time. And now I have to eat crow with Jackie and call my shrink. And my new blouse is ruined.

"How did it go, Keeva?" Jackie asks, looking worried.

"Let's pretend you are President Clinton and I am in the military."

"What? I'm confused," says Jackie.

"Don't ask don't tell."


Later on that afternoon after taking my walk of shame out of the restaurant I sit at my desk contemplating why I really went off on Amos and Jazzmine at the restaurant and why he really walked out on me. As I sit there in a stupor I hear a knock on the door.

"Who is it?" I say thinking maybe Amos has come after me for round two.

"It's me Ms. Keeva," Sophia says with a hesitant voice.

After I breathe a sigh of relief because I wasn't ready for another round I say, "Come in honey. What brings you here today? I thought you were helping Jackie get ready for camp."

"That didn't take too long," Sophia says tangling her hair around her finger in what I know is a nervous gesture.

"What the heck are you so nervous about? You are the most self-assured 16 year old I know."

"I need to ask you a huge favor Ms. Keeva. I know it's last minute but I am in a group called GEMs and this Saturday we are looking for a speaker to discuss positive self-images and professionalism."

"What does GEMs mean?"

"It means Girls Emerging in Modern Society. There are twenty of us and we are all trying to maintain our integrity, intelligence, and have taken a vowel of abstinence."

"And you want me to come? To be honest I am struggling especially in the professionalism and abstinence area. Why don't you ask Jackie or Tiffany to come?"

"Because I want you Ms. Keeva. You represent everything we aspire to be. You are stupid smart, you're paid, you got mad degrees, no rugrats, you aren't hemmed up, and you got swagger!"

"Can you please speak English Sophia?"

"Sorry Ms. Keeva. What I man is you are intelligent, have a great business, are educated, and are single with no kids, and you dress really nice. You know I love Coach Jackie but I emulate you. I tell my friends all the time how much I love working for you."

"What time is the meeting Saturday?"

"Its from ten until twelve and we want you to speak for an hour followed by a Q&A."

"What happens after my session?"

"We bring lunches from home and sit and do strategic planning. Most of the girls are on a tight budget so we keep it pretty simple."

"How about I spring for lunch this Saturday along with hanging out with you during your planning session. Maybe I can help with some of the plans."

"Oh Ms. Keeva, you would do that? The session is enough but buying lunch and hanging out with us is the bomb!" Wait until I tell the girls," Sophia says turning to leave."

"Hold up swole up! How about we keep the lunch between the two of us?"

"Another reason why I love you so much. See you Saturday at the Hadley Park Community Center."

As Sophia walks out the door I pick up the phone and dial Jackie's number.

"Hey Keeva, what's up?"

"Sophia asked me to come speak to 20 girls this Saturday."

"That's great Keeva!"

"What's so great about it girly?"

"You are an amazing person and will connect well with the girls."

"I ain't no role model Jackie! I have made a lot of mistakes and screwed up a lot of people's lives."

"Alright Charles Barkley. Let's take a minute to discuss your greatness. You are a successful business owner who came from the Andrew Jackson projects through Tennessee State University to Vanderbilt University. You are a law abiding citizen most of the time. You are a homeowner, love the Lord and are loyal to your family and friends. Not to mention you are disease free, baby free and drama..."

"But what the hell do I say to those girls?"

"Tell them about your life and experiences. All the lessons you learned and give them tips on how to succeed."

"But I have made so many mistakes! Why didn't she ask you to come and speak?"

"You haven't made any more mistakes than anyone else. And Sophia adores you and emulates you to an extent. I swear sometimes she is you. For someone perceived so confident I am amazed at your lack of confidence sometimes. You have a few days to define your success. And you will find much like Mr. Barkley your 'I'm not a role model' speech will bring more intrigue and attention. Just think about it, even the most devious people have followers. Just use your powers for good and not evil. And not just for the GEMs but also for Amos."

"Says you and my Shrink."

"Tell them your story Keeva. You don't need to practice or write a speech. Just speak from your heart."

"Even the jacked up parts?"

"Talk to them about the jacked up parts and the good stuff. They need to see that you are human and flawed. Show them it doesn't take super powers to be fabulous."

"I tell you, I have spoken to CEOs, CFOs, politicians, and celebrities but I have never been so nervous about speaking to teenage girls!"

"You don't have any problems talking to A.J., Sophia, or Noah. It's the same audience but without as much testosterone."

"Will you go with me please?" Keeva says in a small voice.

"Nope boo! If I go I will steal your shine. I know I got swagger. Now you need to believe the same and knock it out of the park."

"But Jackie-"

"Bye Felicia!"

"No you didn't just revert back to the move *Friday!*"

"OK then, how about just go out there and Shoot the Lights Out!"

"Yeah I know, and don't stink up the gym!"

# Both Hands and Both Feet

The last week has been pretty torturous. Although I'm still a little angry with Keeva, I know I need to talk with her brother Bo to see if I can get a little more insight into what makes her tick. I've been around Bo a few times at some family events and he's come to a few games with Leo, so I know he is a talker.

You would never guess that Bo and Keeva are brother and sister because there is no resemblance. Bo is over six feet tall, a little portly, and brown skinned. He is the blue collar to Keeva's corporate America, the ghetto to her bougie. I teasingly asked Keeva one day if they have the same father, and by the time she finished cleaning my clock I knew without a doubt that they were definitely two halves of a twisted whole. Although they can shred each other to pieces, they always have each other's back. Truly a case of strange love.

I decide to step away from Keeva after the scene in the restaurant so cooler heads could prevail. In the meantime, I call Bo and ask him to meet me for a few beers.

"Hey Amos, man. Leo and I were wondering when you were finally going to take your boy out on the town. It's about time, playa!"

"I was thinking the same thing, Bo. I figure it's time we get to know each other, since I have been dating your sister."

Bo almost spit his beer on me. "You call the shit you two are doing dating? I thought you were just part of the team. Not that I mind, since I thought you could hook your boy up with some season tickets."

"Whoa, man, pump your brakes. How about we work on tickets to a few games, first?"

"What's it worth to you Amos?"

"Come again bro?"

"How many games is it worth for the information you want on my sister?"

"Oh, I see. You think I need to pay to spend more time with Keeva?"

"Come on Amos, I ain't stupid. You want to spend more than just time with Keeva. I've seen that look before. The difference this time is my baby sister has the same look, which is crazy. But I get it. I've done the research. Word on the street is you gonna feed the needy, you got a nut farm in Georgia, and you just signed a fat contract with the Trailblazers. And now you want to take one of the baddest chicks off the market."

I sense that correcting Bo will lengthen this already painful meeting, so I just nod my head yes and wave the waiter over to order another beer.

"I have been anticipating this little chat for a while, so I want you to know that any man who can get my sister to do anything is damn special. She's different around you, in a good way."

"So, you're cool with me moving toward some permanency with Keeva?"

"If you're asking for my permission to move to the next phase, you have my blessing."

"So you are good with us moving forward?"

"Damn man, yes, you can have her hand. In fact, you can have both hands and both feet. But keep in mind that as your future brother-in-law I expect to have some damn good seats, all the nuts I want, and when I'm hungry add me to the free cheese route, you dig?"

"Oh, I most definitely dig."

"Well, welcome to the family. Now give me some love."

So we hug and I get the hell out of dodge before Bo asks me to give him the farm!

***

"Why do I have to go, Rena?"

"How about a little cheese to go with that whine? Why, you ask? Because this is your job in the company, and you're the one who started this with the Tennessee Trailblazers. News has spread about how you helped Ramsey Knight."

"I am sick of football players. I wish Adaris and Shelley had never started this crap."

"Sick of football players, or one in particular? A great way to get over one man is to see a whole bunch of other men. And we really need you to check on Max and Chris, so tag, you're it."

"I'll go, Rena, but I'm flying first class, will stay at the Waldorf Astoria, eat at the Red Rooster, and I'm going to a Broadway play."

"First class, Waldorf, and the Red Rooster are a go. That's all close to where Chris lives anyway. But the Broadway play is on you. I can't get the accountant to write that one off . . . unless you take a client. Now, have a safe trip and call me when you have an update."

***

"So let's go over this one more time Adaris."

"I need you to stop tripping. The only person who really needs to know what is going on is you. Rena and Jackie did their part. They got Keeva on a plane headed to New York to do a seminar for Chris's team. She also plans to do a little shopping and see a play. Since the girls haven't heard from Max, she's going to try to track down World. I keep telling Jackie that things are fine, but she won't listen."

"How do you know things are fine? I'm the most sensitive dude you know, but most of you bottle things up, which is why you won't live as long as me."

"Just because World hasn't mentioned Max in a while doesn't mean something is wrong."

"See, even you think something could be up. You sent the right person to check on him. If anyone can get him to talk it's Keeva. I'm sure she's mad as hell at me right now, so she's the perfect one to check on them."

"I hope this entire trip doesn't backfire in all of our faces. Between you and Keeva and World and Max, our little group is about to self-destruct."

"I hope by the time I get there Saturday evening to surprise Keeva we'll be on our way to recovery. We have a lot to work through, but I need her to think I've been angry with her over the last few weeks so I could put my plan together."

"Needed her to think. Hell, you were angry."

"I was angry because Keeva doesn't trust the way I feel about her. But, come to think about it, she doesn't trust most people. Hence the problem with Jazzmine."

"So how does a good looking young football player work around those issues?"

"We'll do it together. We'll talk to a counselor and try to work through our issues. I can't change the reputation athletes have but I can change her perception of me."

"But you gotta tell her everything, Hunt. Lay it all out on the table. It's hard to discuss our family, our past, and our mistakes, but once you do that you'll feel much better."

"That's one of the reasons I took Keeva home with me. I wanted to be as transparent as I could."

"But you left out a vital detail, Hunt."

"I know man. I will tell her this weekend."

"Go handle your business, but get your ass back here by Monday morning for practice."

"You're retired, Dair. How in the hell you goin' tell me when to come and go on my own football team?"

"Because Shelley doesn't like you as much as I do, so get yo drunk in love ass back or expect a hefty fine."

\*\*\*

The next day I get my butt on a plane, land at JFK airport, and take a cab across the river to the Giant's stadium. I don't understand why everything happened so last minute. But Rena and I can't afford to turn down the chance to work with another NFL team. It can be difficult for a company owned and operated 100 percent by black females to establish working relationships like this, so we have to take advantage of this opportunity.

As soon as I walk into the conference room I start looking around for Chris. I know this class isn't mandatory, but since Chris is an investor in the company that got me the gig, I expect to see him. I spend about three hours with the 15 players who do show up, and it's surprisingly productive. This group is much more intimate and the questions more frank and faster paced than my meeting with the Trailblazers. There's an obvious difference between how northerners and southerners communicate, even among football players. I actually respond better to the Giants players' cut-to-the-chase attitude.

I wrap up the meeting, then hang out for a while to take a few more questions and make some follow-up appointments. I can easily envision this work with football players taking over my life. I make a mental note to talk to Rena about getting Kyle and the rest of our crew up to speed so I can have a backup in the near future.

But now it's me time! I head back to my suite at the Waldorf to take a long hot shower, order dinner from room service, and rest up for my shopping trip. I hope to see Chris and Max tomorrow and have a great dinner with them. Unfortunately the only play I wanted to see was sold out months ago. In the back of my mind I'm considering giving my old friend Kwame a call for a Saturday evening nightcap . . .

***

"Hello."

"Jackie, I need your help!"

"So, when in Rome, huh? No hello or nothing, you just get straight to the point."

"I need Chris' address."

"You didn't see him at the stadium?"

"Girl, it's like Fort Knox in there since 9/11, security is tight as hell. All I know is he was a no show at the meeting."

"Did you try calling him?"

"Stop talking to me like I am stuck on stupid. Of course I called him, I asked around for him—I even tried to get into the locker room. I did find out that he's been showing up just in time for practice or a workout, and then he leaves right after."

"That could mean he's rushing back to Max."

"Or, it could mean he's not. I do know that his teammates are very protective. After I asked a few questions about him I started getting raised eyebrows. I realized I was starting to look like a thirsty groupie so I shut up . . . until I saw the equipment guy."

"And what did he say?"

"I just told you. Don't you have his address from the reception invitations?"

"I have his old address, but remember he closed on his new brownstone in Harlem a few months ago. I never had a reason to ask for it."

"Dammit! Well, do what you gotta do to get it girl and be quick about it!"

"And what do I get . . . you know a girl loves shoes."

"This is your best friend, Jackie. I am trying to help you out!"

"All right, all right. Let me see what I can come up with."

"I suggest you do some rubbing, patting, and sliding."

"You said make it quick. If you are recommending I try the RPS maneuver it won't be quick."

"Stop being nasty—just handle your business, girl!"

***

"Hey babe, what you doing?"

"Going over my business plan. It's time for us to submit a final plan to Game Changers. I still can't believe they suggested we assume the same name with all rights and privileges," Adaris says as he watches Jackie move across the room. "What you doing?"

"Nothing. Just checking on you. Can I get you anything?" Jackie asks as she sits on Adaris' lap.

"Just you, baby. Now, what is it you want—I know that look on your face."

Jackie moves her hand down Adaris' thigh and leans over to kiss him on the neck. As she starts to unbutton his shirt, he leans further back in the chair.

"Have I told you today how much I love you?"

"Umm . . . I would rather you show me," Adaris says, grabbing Jackie's butt to pull her more snugly against him.

"Then you'll give me anything I want?" Jackie says as she slowly grinds against Adaris' lap.

"Um hmm . . . anything baby."

More than a few minutes later, as Adaris lies sprawled across his office desk with Jackie on top, both of them naked as the day they were born, Jackie continues the conversation she started some time ago.

"Are you ready to give me what I want, baby?"

"I thought I just did," Adaris says, reaching up to kiss Jackie.

"I need Chris' address."

"Why?"

"While Keeva is up in New York she's going to check on him and Max."

"Why?"

"Because we have been trying to call Max for the last two weeks and she isn't answering her phone!"

"I told you I talked to Chris the other day."

"Did you ask him about Max?"

"No, but we usually don't talk about our ladies."

"Adaris Singleton, you know that is a lie. You guys gossip more than we do."

Adaris holds back a huge grin. "Our talk is a little more caveman, baby. We don't get into feelings or emotions because we think it makes us look like punks."

"Well, while you all are pounding your chests, we are worried about our girl. Now, Chris is the last person who saw her or talked to her, and I don't want to call and worry Mrs. Hilton if it turns out Max isn't back on the island."

"Jackie, if Chris and Max are having issues, it's not our business to intervene. Just like our business is ours."

"We don't want to intervene. We just want to make sure Max is ok. Please baby, just let Keeva do that while she is in New York."

"I swear, you can convince me to do any damn thing. But this is it. After you find out that Max is ok, I want you to stay out of it. The last thing I want is for any issues they may have to cause us any problems. "

Jackie leans over to give Adaris a lingering kiss. "Thank you baby. And I promise, this is it."

As Adaris goes to get Chris' address, he mumbles under his breath, "Anyone who says women can't seduce men into doing anything has no clue about the power of the booty."

***

After I ring the doorbell for about five minutes, the door finally swings open. "What the hell are you doing ringing my damn doorbell, Keeva?"

I give Chris a long look up and down, and I am stunned. His hair clearly hasn't been cut for weeks, his five o'clock shadow is more like midnight, his eyes are bloodshot, and he smells like moonshine.

"Well hello, Chris. It's good to see you too. By the way, you look awful and you smell worse."

"You haven't answered my question."

I peer around Chris to see if I can catch a glimpse of Max. "You know why I'm here, Chris. Where the hell is Max?"

"Not that it's any of your damn business, but she isn't here."

"Then where is she?"

"Hell if I know!"

"Well, when did she leave?"

"Look, Max is your girl. If she hasn't called to tell you where she is, that is her business. Now, you can get the fuck off my stoop, and don't show up again without calling me first."

I step as close as I can to Chris without further offending my already offended senses.

"Chris, you can use all those damn cuss words to intimidate most people, but I ain't that girl. I am pretty sure whatever happened between you and my girl does not outweigh the fact that we hope she is somewhere safe, so don't get it twisted. Now, I will leave, but if I find out you did anything to put her in harm's way, I will come back and personally beat your ass my damn self!"

"Well, get in line Keeva, because I am kicking my own ass right about now. And if you want the two of us to keep any semblance of a friendship, I suggest you stop insinuating that I did anything to Max."

"Oh, go to hell Chris!"

"I am already there, Keeva!"

I'm still not sure if Chris knows anything about the baby and I don't want to say anything to get Max in any further trouble, so I give Chris a stare down, suck my teeth, and start walking down the stairs. By the time I hit the second step he slams the door so hard I almost trip. As I walk down the street and hail a cab to the Red Rooster, I send Jackie and Serena a terse text.

*Just left Chris' pad. Max has been 86-ed and Chris looks like death warmed over. Jackie, it's time to call Mrs. Hilton to check on our girl. There is definitely trouble in paradise. I need a drink! TTYL*

By the time I arrive at the Red Rooster for my seven o'clock reservation, I'm exhausted and worried. I knew that Chris had a football persona, but off the field he is fantastic. For him to look and feel the way he does, I'm guessing the pregnancy announcement didn't go over well. But why? The two of them clearly love each other. I guess sometimes love just isn't enough—I am living testimony of that. As I process my conversation with Chris, I realize that although Chris looked angry, his eyes looked like he was devastated. I keep racking my brain to try to figure out what the hell could have happened—why would make Max fall off the face of the earth and make Chris look like someone died. Wait a minute, did someone die? My over-active imagination starts to think about Jeffrey Dahmer and Charles Manson. And then I send another text to Jackie and Serena.

*Call Mrs. Hilton, stat. I don't have a good feeling right now. Someone text me back ASAP.*

By the time I send the text the hostess is ready to usher me to a table. I sit down and immediately order a shot of Tequila to calm my nerves. By the time I'm about to take the second shot, my phone dings, making me jump right out of my seat. I nervously pick up my phone and read the message.

*Talked to Mrs. Hilton and Max is back on the island. She is ok, but all is not well. Mrs. Hilton doesn't know what is going on.*

"Waitress. Another shot please!"

"Don't you think you need to slow down?"

"I have got to be hallucinating—I can't be hearing Amos' voice," I mumble to myself as I rest my head on my hand. "I should have got my ass on the first thing smoking back to Tennessee."

"Yes, you probably should have, but I decided to come and fly back with you."

And then I look up . . . way up and into the smiling eyes of Amos Hunter. "What the hell are you doing here?"

"I came to talk to you."

"Let's see . . . you won't return my calls or my texts in Tennessee but you'll fly all the way up to New York to talk?"

"Actually, I don't want to do any serious talking right now. Let's have dinner, and then I have some surprises for you."

"Surprises? What makes you think I want any surprises? I have had enough surprises to last me a lifetime. First Max, then Tiffany, then Aunt Ella and the Dasher. I tell you what, why don't you surprise me by apologizing for making a damn fool out of me over the last few weeks." In my half drunken stupor I realize that this isn't the first time Amos has seen me in this condition. Then I take a good long look at him. He's wearing a lovely tan linen suit with a starched white shirt and a pale green tie. On his feet he's wearing brown Ferragamo closed-toe sandals. And he smells heavenly. But, I refuse to come undone because the man I thought was down for me like two flat tires has miraculously shown up for dinner!

"No more tequila for you," Amos says, slipping the next shot out of my hand. "I came up here to say I am sorry, and I want us to move past this and enjoy our evening here. I know we have a lot to clear up, but can we just enjoy dinner and the rest of the evening first? I promise you, we will talk."

Just as I'm about to shoot back a rebuttal, the waiter comes over and says, "Mr. Hunter, Mr. Samuelsson has your tasting menu ready if you would like to be seated."

"Keeva, are we ok to proceed with dinner?"

"Only if you tell me Marcus is coming out sometime during our dinner to meet me. Jackie is going to die when I tell her about this."

"Yes, he will come out to meet us later on. Now, can we proceed?"

With a small sniff I give my approval, and we proceed with a five-course tasting that is to die for. We keep the conversation light and low key. My stewing is down to a low simmer, and I decide to let Amos' apology stand—for now. When we finish the meal, the world renowned chef Marcus Samuelson comes out to meet us, and after a few minutes of high praise and a photo op, we're on our way to the next stop.

We step out to a waiting limousine. "So what is this surprise you mentioned earlier?"

"Front row seats to *A Raisin in the Sun* at the Barrymore Theatre."

"You are taking me to see my baby's daddy? How did you know I wanted to see Denzel?"

"You've been talking about this play since you heard it was coming out. And now you need to eat a little crow and take back what you said to Chris earlier. He pulled some strings to help me set this up."

"So you heard about our little chat? I will apologize for the go to hell comment, but not for looking for Max."

"I don't blame you for checking on Max, but whatever is going on with the two of them, you need to stay out of it Keeva."

"Now that I have confirmed that Max is safely back in St. Croix I will leave it alone, but if I find out Chris hurt my girl—"

"Like I said babe, stay out of it. We have a lot to discuss ourselves, but for now will you just-"

"I know, just be. Oh, I will be for my baby, but after this play you better BE ready to talk."

***

After the play we head back to the hotel.

"Thanks for a wonderful evening, Amos. Now can we talk so you can head back to your hotel?"

"I'm staying in the same hotel as you."

"Really, what room?"

"2246."

"Hey, that's Uncle Shorty's birthday. Remind me to play that number tomorrow. I'm in 2248. You wanna tell me how you did that?"

"Patience baby," Amos says as we head to my room.

As soon as I open the door I round on Amos and say, "Explain to me why you were so upset with me at the restaurant two weeks ago?"

"I could sense from the moment you came to the table that you wouldn't listen to a word I said."

"What did you expect, Amos? I see you at a nice restaurant with the woman I think is gunning for you. How should I have handled it?"

"You have male friends, Keeva, and your line of work is very male dominated. I wouldn't have made an assumption before talking to you."

"That is correct, but my friends don't show up everywhere I am—weddings, football games, cancer walks."

"Jazzmine and I run in the same circles. And it's bull to think that men and women can't have platonic relationships."

"Did the friendship become platonic before or after you found out you were kissing cousins?"

"Be careful darling. I am pretty sure you don't want to play truth or dare, or a lot of skeletons may fall out of your closet."

"Are you saying I am promiscuous?"

"Hell no and I'm not interested in any of the punks you dated. But if you start asking me, turnabout is fair play."

"So you won't answer my question?"

"I did, Keeva, you just didn't listen, which is why I walked out of the restaurant a few weeks ago."

"I have an issue with men deserting me, and that day at the restaurant you did just that! Fuss at me, talk to me, but don't dismiss me just because you set things up to look like I was in the wrong. No, I shouldn't have made any assumptions, but you should have told me what was going on, Amos!"

"Having a disagreement is not a dismissal Keeva. You blew everything out of proportion, and to keep from telling you something that would hurt your feelings, it was best for me to leave."

"So you took your damn ball and went home? I never thought you were a runner, Amos."

"That's your problem, Keeva. It's you against the world. When are you going to realize that some things require you to wait a minute? Everything doesn't require or deserve an immediate response. Don't you give media trainings about just that? You spend all this time counseling and telling people what to do, but you don't listen! Now, if you want to be with me you will need to realize that there will be some give and take. It's not always about how *you* feel!"

"Oh yes it is, because I am always alone!"

"You're living in a self-inflicted exile. And if you want to be with me you need to get out of it. I am a man, Keeva, and I refuse to allow you to emasculate me! If we are going to be together you need to learn that I am the man and you are the woman. I need a strong woman who can stand beside, behind, and in front of me. I have three more years in the league, tops and then I will move home to assume the CEO position of Hunt's Nuts. I need a woman who is down for me."

"CEO?"

Amos starts walking toward me and says, "Yes, dammit, CEO. And I need a CEW, Keeva. A chief executive wife, not a sparring partner. Put your damn dukes down, woman!"

"What did you just say?"

"I said put your dukes down, baby."

"No, before the dukes part, Mr. CEO."

"Oh, the wife part. Yes Keeva. I flew all the way up here to propose to you."

"But you just said I have trust issues. Why do you want to marry someone who doesn't trust you?"

"Oh, you trust me. You just don't trust marriage. And that's ok. That's why we'll do pre-marital counseling until we both feel we're ready. I knew that day that we rode to your home in the limousine that you were going to be special to me."

Just then there's a knock at the door, and I suddenly remembered that I invited my friend Kwame up for a nightcap

"Before you finish your proposal, I need to tell you something Amos."

"Don't you want me to get the door first?" Amos says with a sly smile.

"Speaking of trust issues, I need to tell you that my friend Kwame was coming to see me this evening to hang out."

"Hang out like Jazz and me hang out, or hang out like knocking boots hang out?"

"Just hang out and catch up, I promise."

"Well, in that case, let me open the door for our room service. I sent that shrimp Kwame away when I came by earlier. And you should be glad that he said the same thing as you or I would be having trust issues as well."

Amos opens the door with a flourish and the waiter enters pushing a cart on which are sitting a dozen red roses, a bottle of champagne, and three covered dishes.

"Babe, we just had dinner. What is all of this? Don't you want to get back to my proposal?"

Amos bends down on one knee and pulls me to sit on the other one, and then he says, "As I was saying, I love you Keeva. I want you to be my wife, to have my babies, and to grow old together. I want to take care of you, and I want you to take care of me. Will you marry me Keeva?"

"Are you sure? I can be difficult to get along with, and . . . "

"I'll take the good and the bad, Keeva, and we will find someone to help us with our issues."

"That may mean a long engagement, Amos," I say with a sigh, as I curiously peer over his shoulder to look at the covered dishes on the cart.

"Don't you want to see what's under the cover?"

"Not really. I'm more interested in you finishing up the proposal."

"After you choose what you want to eat."

"Really I can wait—"

"Keeva, do as I ask, please!"

"Fine, but I'm not hungry," I huff as I grab the first cover off the dish. And then for the first time in God knows when, I am speechless. Sitting in the middle of a plate is a ring box with a gorgeous 4 carat oval diamond ring, with small baguettes on the side.

"I figured that would shut you up. I wasn't sure which ring you wanted, so I selected three for you to choose from."

I quickly uncover the other two dishes and almost pass out. The second dish has an even larger pear shaped solitaire ring, surrounded by two emerald green trillion shaped stones. The other ring is a thick platinum band surrounded by round and emerald shaped diamonds.

"Oh Amos! They are all beautiful and so unique. Did you pick them all out?"

"Yes baby, I did. Now you choose."

"How many can I pick?"

With a guffaw Amos says, "You can choose one, and I'll let you help me design your wedding band."

I stand there with my mouth wide open and tears in my eyes. Amos gathers me in his arms and leans down to say, "During this whole courtship I have always wanted you to think less and follow your heart more. Stop thinking about the age difference, the size difference, and trying to protect yourself. You gave me your heart, and I sho nuf gave you mine, so let's take care of each other. Now make your choice, and don't over analyze it," Amos says, kissing me on the crown of my head and walking me closer to the table.

I lean over and the pear-shaped ring beckons me. I lean over, grab it, and give it to Amos to place on my third finger, left hand. As he slides it on, I know it's perfect for me.

"You remembered that the emerald is my favorite stone?"

"Of course. And I knew you'd pick this one. Take it off and read the inscription."

I slide it off and peer inside. It says, "Mrs. Keeva Hunter."

"When we consummate our vows you will assume my name and my name only."

As I stand there staring into his eyes, I realize that dropping my surname Hudson and my exes name McGhee is a sign that I'm letting go of my past and putting all my faith, hope, and trust in my future.

Amos picks me up and starts walking toward the bed to end what will be the first of many meetings. He puts me down and says, "You haven't said 'yes' yet Keeva."

As I stare down at my ring and back into Amos' eyes, I say, "Oh, the answer is definitely yes, but answer one question for me," I say looping my arms around his neck.

"Anything."

"Do you plan to return to the farm in Macon after you retire from football?"

"Why do you ask that babe?"

"Because I cannot wait to become a farmer's wife and raise our children on the farm."

"Well in that case I plan to retire after I complete the three year contract I just signed with the Trailblazers. But only if you promise that we can start having babies before the contract runs out."

"How about we start practicing after the wedding and see what we can come up with by year three?"

Made in the USA
Charleston, SC
03 December 2015